CLOSER!

Jess Watkins realises that she's a dreamer with no ambitions when her friend Becky gets married. However, she manages to land herself a job as secretary at the Brachan Window Company. Her boss, Jared King, makes a big impression on her — and not just professionally. But she finds that Jared is married to Suzanne. Then, her career begins to blossom, although the office seems in danger of closing. Working in a double-dealing world, can Jess ever find true love?

Books by Julia Douglas
in the Linford Romance Library:

NASHVILLE CINDERELLA

JULIA DOUGLAS

◆

CLOSER!

Complete and Unabridged

LINFORD
Leicester

First published in Great Britain in 2011

First Linford Edition
published 2012

British Library CIP Data

Douglas, Julia.
 Closer!. - -
 (Linford romance library)
 1. Love stories.
 2. Large type books.
 I. Title II. Series
 823.9'2–dc23

 ISBN 978–1–4448–1034–9

Published by
F. A. Thorpe (Publishing)
Anstey, Leicestershire

Set by Words & Graphics Ltd.
Anstey, Leicestershire
Printed and bound in Great Britain by
T. J. International Ltd., Padstow, Cornwall

This book is printed on acid-free paper

1

'I don't know why you didn't just stick with Leo!' Of course, that was easy for Becky to say — radiant in her going away dress and about to fly half way around the world on her honeymoon.

Jess wouldn't have admitted it, but as she sat on the church pew earlier and watched Becky sweep by in her dazzling white confection, she had indeed found herself thinking how easily that could have been her, standing in front of the smiling vicar, saying 'I do'. She'd felt a similar wistful twinge when her other friend, Ellie, got hitched a few months before.

But it was the sun through the stained glass that made her eyes go blinky and blurry. It was the organ music, the wedding cake dress and the church bells that gave her lower lip the wobbles . . . not the memory of Leo himself. Jess found it hard to explain why. After all, he was good looking, kind — he wouldn't be hard to 'stick with.' But, as usual, Jess hadn't let things with Leo even get off the ground.

'Where were the trumpets?' She heard herself almost shouting to Becky, above the happy din of the reception. 'Where was that bolt from the blue that knocks you off your feet?'

'You sound more like you want to be struck by lightning!' Becky laughed.

'Isn't that what everyone wants?' Jess asked. Hadn't it been like that for Becky? She wanted to ask, but a noisy wedding reception on the dot of midnight was no place for a heart to heart. Becky had a hundred and one well-wishers vying for her attention and a whole new life waiting for her in a vintage Rolls Royce outside.

The last thing Jess heard Becky say, before she was swept away in the crowd was, 'You're a dreamer, Jess! I don't think you know what you want!'

It was said laughingly, but as Jess was

left standing alone, champagne glass in hand, amid the partying crowd, the words stung her like a slap.

She was still thinking about them the next day. And, being man-less on a Sunday, she had plenty of time to dwell. Becky, of course, had always known what she wanted, and she'd always got it: the man, the car, the career. Jess had always been her unambitious friend, the one who made Becky shine. She didn't mind. Becky was fun and she enjoyed the little bit of glamour that rubbed off on her. Jess was content to sit on the sidelines and dream — if Becky had to put it like that.

But what was wrong with dreaming? she eventually consoled herself. Did it matter if you didn't have every area of your life planned out like a bus schedule? She may look like a hopeless underachiever compared with Becky, but she was only twenty-two. She was hardly dreaming her life away.

★ ★ ★

She felt differently on Monday, when she woke up cold and late and thought of Becky, cuddled up with hubby in Barbados. Half an hour later, she was hurrying along a gritty high street, her feet cramped by her shoes, uncomfortable in a cheap office suit and late for an interview for yet another dead end job. Dreams might keep you warm, but they didn't pay the rent.

The address wasn't promising. Up an alley beside a betting shop, he said. It sounded a bit dodgy, really, but she liked the sound of the voice on the phone. Well spoken and precise, but not posh, it was the confident voice of a man who had made his own way in life. He sounded strong, solid and trustworthy. He was formal and businesslike, but not unkind, Jess thought. He had an interesting name, too. Jared King.

The narrow alley led her to a small yard jammed with cars; mostly bangers but a couple of flash ones, including two big black BMWs. Close to the mouth of the passage, an open door was set into the back wall of the betting shop. A dirty brown staircase led up into the gloom. There was no sign, but it had to be the place.

Taking a last lungful of morning air, Jess clattered up the bare treads. At the top was a closed door with a small metal sign screwed to it: Brachan Window Company. Through the door, Jess recognised the voice from the phone, Jared King. It was just his voice, occasionally pausing, never answered, as if he were giving a lecture, rather than having a conversation. He sounded forceful, dominant and just the teeniest aggressive. Jess felt her heart beginning to pound. It was just like all those mornings in her school days, arriving late at the assembly hall door and hearing the headmaster droning on inside. Prising herself out of bed in the morning was something she'd never been good at.

Well, she could either knock or open it. She wasn't going to wait out here and be even later. The voice wasn't the sort she felt like interrupting with a knock, so she took a deep breath, turned the door knob and gave it a push. The door moved six inches before jarring against something solid — which turned out to be the back of a very tall and gangly teenager wearing a dark suit. He stuck a hard and spotty face around the door and glared at her.

'Sorry!' Jess yelped.

Grudgingly, he moved just far enough away from the door that Jess was able to slip through into the room. She couldn't move further because the room was packed with people, all of them standing and facing away from her towards the currently hidden from view Jared who, thankfully, hadn't stopped talking.

' . . . the important thing to ensure is both decision makers will be there . . . '

Jess was glad she'd worn a charcoal skirt suit — the crowd looked like they'd come from a funeral. Her relief at slipping in unnoticed was quickly replaced by a frustration that she couldn't see what was going on. She edged her way around the crowd in the hope of finding a better view.

She still couldn't see, but as she reached the dirty sash windows overlooking the high street she became uncomfortably aware of how hot and airless the overcrowded room was.

'Just ask them straight,' Jared was saying. ''Will your husband or wife be there?' If not, ask, 'When will you both be home?''

Jess didn't have a clue what he was talking about. But she knew that if she didn't open one of those windows and get some fresh air into her lungs she was going to pass out.

Not wanting to draw attention to herself, she tried to lift the nearest window sash just a little, but it might as well have been nailed down. Feeling trapped, she put her back into the task, but it wouldn't budge. Becoming desperate, she strained with all her might.

'UUURGH!' Jess exclaimed, like a weightlifter, as the sash flew upwards and rammed into the upper casing with a bang that shook the room.

Gasping with relief, Jess sucked in air like a landed fish — until she realised that the voice behind her had stopped abruptly. Slowly, she turned to find that everyone in the room was staring at her. She only saw one of them, though, because all the dark-suited young people had parted like the Red Sea to create a funnel-shaped passage that focused all of Jess's attention on her first sight of Jared King.

Her breathing stopped. Her heart nearly did, too.

He was standing behind a desk and in front of a blackboard, a stick of chalk poised in one hand. It was a big hand and he was a big man. The cut of his grey pinstriped waistcoat and the shimmering silk of an expensive-looking shirt emphasised the muscular width of his shoulders.

The intensity of his gaze nailed Jess to the window sill as surely as if she'd been struck by a thunderbolt. For a long moment he studied her, unsmiling, as if she were a butterfly in a case. Eventually, one of his eyebrows rose slowly and he said, levelly, 'And you are . . . ?'

Jess remembered to start breathing.

'Jess,' she squeaked. 'I mean, Jessica. Jessica Watkins. I've come about the job.'

'The canvassing job?'

'No, the admin job. Sales support.'

'Well, in that case Miss Jess-I-mean-Jessica-Jessica Watkins . . . ' — Jared directed a smirk at a tall blond man in a blue suit, who was standing to the right of his desk — ' . . . if you'd like to take a seat, I'll be with you shortly. Now, if I may continue . . . ?'

The crowd turned back to the front and the sea of suits closed up again, so that Jess's view of Jared was blocked once more. As they turned away, the blond sidekick broke into a toothy grin at her expense, which was picked up as a series of smiles and sniggers by the rest of the assembled.

But Jess barely noticed. Rooted to the spot, she had a crazy impulse to phone Becky in Barbados and say, 'Remember what I was saying about trumpets and thunderbolts . . . ?'

She'd never seen a man so commanding. It wasn't just that he was older than everyone else in the room by a good ten years, nor that he was so solidly built, or expensively dressed. He gave off an aura of such calm inner certainty about who he was and where he stood in the world that Jess felt weak at the knees.

Of course, it was a shame he'd taken the mickey out of her. But as she sank gratefully into a rather nasty green office chair, she decided she'd at least go through the interview before passing judgement on him as a nice or nasty boss. She'd heard about these macho sales environments. Maybe he was just testing her, to see what she was made of.

With a light-headed inward giggle, she decided he'd have to work harder than that to get rid of her. Besides, although the glare he'd given her was far from friendly, she thought she detected a twinkly softness in his eyes that suggested he wasn't quite the tough nut he clearly liked to appear.

' . . . remember the three Cs,' he was saying, 'Close, close, close . . . '

Jess closed her eyes and enjoyed the sound of his voice. It was firm and authoritative but definitely not unkind. It was a sound she could get used to.

She was just beginning to think that the morning was seriously perking up, when she was shaken out of her thoughts by the urgent clang of a fire bell and an outbreak of shouting.

For a second, Jess thought she'd dozed off, and fallen straight into a nightmare. But the noise shaking her to her core was far too vivid for that. Leaping from her chair, she expected to see the room on fire. But although the shouting continued unabated, nobody was hurrying towards the door. Instead of sounding panicky, they sounded happy.

As astonishment overwhelmed her initial shock, she realised Jared was shaking a big brass hand-bell as violently as he could, while shouting, 'Who's the best?' over and over again. In response, the blond man was leading everyone else in a repeated cheer of, 'We are!'

On and on, it went: 'Who's the best?' Clang, clang, clang! 'We are!'

Just when Jess thought she was about to be driven completely mad or deaf or both, the ringing abruptly stopped.

'Go on then!' Jared shouted, 'Get out there and bring me leads!'

Certain that she'd walked into a madhouse, Jess flopped back onto the swivel chair — which subsided below her with a loud squeak — while all the suited men and women jostled and joked their way out of the room.

As the last of their footsteps echoed up the stairs, Jared strode across a well-worn orange carpet and thrust out his hand.

'Sorry about that,' he smiled. 'I'm Jared King.'

Jess took the big hand Jared King offered. It completely enveloped her own, but in a surprisingly soft and gentle way. It was a reassuring handshake that said here was a rock you could anchor yourself to if the waters of the world got choppy. That was exactly what Jess needed at that moment. After all that bell-ringing she felt quite dizzy.

'I don't suppose you supply earplugs?' she asked.

Jared laughed. It was an easy, relaxed laugh and as Jess looked up into his big, handsome face she saw, in an instant, that he didn't have an unkind bone in his body.

His laugh was echoed by another man's chuckle, and Jess turned to see that the blond man in the blue suit hadn't left with the others. There were several desks around the edges of the room, all of them pushed tightly against the wall to create the maximum standing space in the centre, and the blond man was standing in front of one of them, loading a leather file into an open briefcase.

Jared led her over, saying, 'This is Carl, our top closer.' She gave Jared a questioning look. 'Salesman,' he explained. 'As in closing the deal.'

'Always closing, never posing, eh, boss?' said Carl. He turned to give Jess the full effect of his leanly handsome face, bright blue eyes and big, pearly grin. 'Pleased to meet you Jess. It is Jess, isn't it, or is it Jessica?' He flashed a grin at Jared as if to say, aren't I clever?

Jess felt her blood boil. 'Jess is fine,' she said, coldly.

'Yes, I can see that,' Carl smirked.

Then, even though he had already been introduced, Carl thrust his hand out and told her his name again. Jess couldn't tell if he wanted to make sure she remembered it, or whether he just enjoyed saying it. He ran his tongue around the word Carl as if it were a piece of chocolate. Jess wondered if you

14

could die from exposure to so much smarminess. But, not wanting to be impolite, she accepted his handshake.

'Don't worry about us, Jess,' Carl said smoothly, 'We all tease each other around here.'

He held her hand, and her eyes, a little longer than she felt comfortable with until Jared cut in with, 'Are you seeing the Hattersleys this morning?'

'Yet again,' Carl grimaced. 'Hopefully this time they'll have decided.'

'I hope so,' said Jared. 'That's one sale we could use.'

Carl checked his watch, which Jess noticed was identical to Jared's. 'Speaking of which, I'll have to love you and leave you, Jess.'

Carl snapped shut his briefcase and hefted it off the desk. It was an expensive-looking case, shiny alligator with bright brass fittings. Like the watches both men wore, and the tailored cut of their suits, Jess thought its opulence looked out of place in the incredibly tatty, beige-painted office.

'Good luck with the interview,' Carl called without a backward glance, as he headed through the door.

'Don't worry about Carl,' said Jared. 'He's full of himself, but that's his job. He's a good kid at heart.'

The 'kid' comment surprised Jess, the way he said it as if he were old enough to be Carl's father, which he wasn't by a long shot. Taking a good look at his face, she put him at about thirty and Carl perhaps twenty-five, although Jared carried himself with the air of a much more mature and experienced man. He looked like he'd grown accustomed to carrying a fair weight of responsibility on his shoulders, although he seemed to relax now, as if he felt the need to play a role as boss when Carl was around.

'So, let me get you a cup of tea,' he suggested.

It felt odd having a boss wait on her and she smiled at the readiness of this big, well dressed man to 'play mum'. Not that 'mum' kept a well-stocked larder. He stepped into a kitchenette off the main office that was no bigger than a cupboard and presently called over his shoulder, 'You don't mind coffee, do you — and black? Only we're out of milk.'

A few minutes later, Jared was sitting in front of his blackboard, a pair of big black, well-polished brogues propped on the corner of his desk, and a steaming mug that bore the legend 'Super Boss', cradled in his lap. Jess perched nervously on a swivel chair on the other side of the desk, acutely aware of how strongly attracted to him she felt, and that they were alone in the room. To hide her nerves, she tightly gripped her mug with both hands. Scared to meet his eyes for too long at a time in case she went all moony, she noticed her mug was chipped and labelled 'Dad'.

'Have you ever worked in a top flight sales environment before?' Jared asked sharply and straight to the point.

'Um, well, not really . . . '

'But you've done word-processing, and you can answer a phone?'

'Of course.'

Jared swung his feet off the desk and leaned forward on his elbows. 'I'm going to be straight with you, Jess. I've had a lot of applications for this job. Some of them have a lot more qualifications and experience than you, but in this game you learn to judge people on character, not bits of paper. I think you'd fit in very well. How would you feel about a week's trial period, starting today, and we'll see how you get on?'

'Today?' Jess tried not to spill her coffee.

'Unless you have other plans.'

'No, of course not,' she gushed.

Jared beamed at her in a way that was so contagious Jess's stomach flipped over. 'That's agreed then. Do you have any questions?'

Jess had a million, but all of them were too personal to ask. So she just grinned, nervously flicked a finger at an

18

instrument she'd never seen on another boss's desk and said, 'What's with the bell?'

Jared leaned back in his chair and laughed. 'Well, you see . . . ' But at that moment the phone began to bleep and he reached for it instinctively. Then he stopped himself, smiled, and raised his eyebrows at Jess, as if to say, *Go on, then*.

Jess's heart quickened; her first task as secretary. Taking a sip of coffee to wet a suddenly dry throat, she picked up the handset. 'Hello . . . ?'

Quick as a flash, Jared thrust a business card in front of her and pointed at the name splashed across the top.

'Brachan Window Company,' Jess added and he gave her a thumbs up.

'Who's that?' A female voice almost bit Jess's ear off.

Taken aback by the hostility, but determined to remain calm, Jess said, 'It's Jess. I mean, Jessica.' Annoyed with herself for sounding so uncertain, she

19

added more smugly, 'I'm the secretary.'

Jared nodded his approval, and she felt herself blushing warmly. The caller, however, was not impressed.

'Is Jared there?' She snapped.

'Er, one moment. May I ask who's calling?'

'Suzanne,' the voice snapped. With an icy note, she added, 'His wife.'

'Oh.' Jess felt her gut convulse as if from a kick. Hiding her reaction she said, 'I'll just put you through.' She pressed the mute button and offered him the phone. 'It's your wife.'

Jared's reaction was not what Jess expected; the smile and colour couldn't have slipped out of his face more quickly if she'd said, *It's the tax man*. Leaning away from the proffered phone, he stood and pulled a mobile out of his trouser pocket. 'Tell her I'll call her on the mobile,' he said, gruffly.

Jess conveyed the information, but received no thanks — Suzanne simply cut the line. Catching her breath, she watched Jared leave the office, keying his phone with his thumb as he went. As his heavy brogues clattered down the bare wooden stairs, she heard him say, 'Suzanne . . . ' in a flat tone, but no more, as he went outside into the yard.

Alone in the unfamiliar office, Jess sagged in her chair. To stop herself falling apart, the sensible side of her started rationalising like crazy. Why on earth should she be shocked to learn he was married? Why would a man like that not be? And who said he'd ever be interested in a girl like her, anyway?

And yet she was so certain she'd heard those trumpets and felt that thunderbolt she'd waited for all her life that she felt like bursting into tears.

But she was also intrigued by Suzanne's hostility, and Jared's reaction to her call. There was definitely something interesting going on there . . .

Stop it, Jess, she chided herself. To get away from the whats and maybes chasing each other in ever faster circles around her head, she forced herself to focus on something concrete. She had a new job. That was good. Her boss was nice. That was double good. Her boss was a hunk. That would be a new experience. Surely that was enough to smile about?

At that moment, a clattering of heavy shoes on the stairs announced Jared's return. He burst into the office looking pumped-up and boss-like.

'Right, to work!' he declared. He pulled a wallet from his back pocket and extracted a tenner. 'You wouldn't nip out and get us some tea, milk and sugar, would you?' He strode across the orange carpet. 'And who left this bloomin' window open? It's freezing in here!'

2

Having a dishy boss didn't stop Jess being late for work. She just lay longer in bed thinking dreamy thoughts about him. At least when she got to the office, she was ready for the bell-ringing this time. Sneaking in behind the crowd and yanking up the sash window, she pulled two clumps of cotton wool out of her pocket and jammed them into her ears just in time.

Jared's pep talk was shorter this morning, and there were only half as many people there to hear it. When they'd finally bustled out — with slightly less enthusiasm than they had yesterday — Jared crossed the room and closed the window.

He gave her a friendly smile, and it was only when she realised she couldn't hear what he was saying, that she remembered she still had the cotton wool in her ears. She pulled it out with an apologetic smile, and asked, 'So, what is it with all the bell-ringing?'

'The two Ms — motivation and morale.' Jared took off his suit jacket, hung it on his chair and perched on the corner of his desk. He pointed at the door. 'That lot are the canvassers, my foot soldiers, the invasion force . . . '

'Is that why there are half as many as there were yesterday?' Jess asked cheekily. 'Because the rest were killed in action?'

Jared pointed at her. 'Got it in one. Monday is our big recruitment day. Most of the people you saw yesterday were here for the first time and a lot of them won't have sold anything before. We send them out onto the streets to knock on doors and make appointments so our closers — the salesmen like Carl — can go in and sell windows.

'It's harder work than most of them expect, so after a day of people telling them where to go, a lot of them simply don't come back. By the end of the

24

week, there will only be one or two left. Those will be the ones who become team leaders and, maybe closers some day. But in the meantime, we need more canvassers, so next Monday, we get another load in and start all over again.'

'You must get through a lot of people,' said Jess.

'Thousands,' said Jared. 'But it's commission only, so it only costs us the price of the advert in the local rag.'

'What on earth does the advert say?'

'On target earnings thirty grand a year!' Jared laughed like it was the biggest joke in the world and Jess couldn't help scowling. Perhaps he saw himself reflected in her eyes, for when his mirth subsided, he looked guilty.

She couldn't stop herself saying, 'You don't think the reason half those people don't come back is because they think it's all a bit nuts? All the bellringing and stuff, I mean.'

Caught off guard, Jared gave her a long, level look, as if wondering if she had a point. Then he half smiled, half sighed, and said, 'Have you got enough work to do?'

★　★　★

Jess had plenty of work to do. The office paperwork looked as if it hadn't been touched in a month and she realised she'd have her work cut out just getting on top of things. She didn't mind, she liked being busy, and although she didn't know the first thing about the way a window company operated, she was a quick typist and had a natural knack for getting things in order.

Luckily Jared was a patient boss and explained things when she asked, said 'please' and 'thank you', never seemed particularly grumpy, praised her work when she did particularly well, and never shouted at her. None of her previous bosses had ticked all those boxes. And not one had been so easy on the eye. The tingle she felt in his presence put a spring in her step that hadn't been there for ages.

After a couple of days, she actually managed to convince herself that the fact he was married wasn't such a bad thing. The strength of her initial feelings for him had scared her and he was so far out of her league it was scarier still. Living in a dream felt safer than hot-blooded reality.

And it was a dream, she reflected with a heavy sigh, when she flopped down on her bed at night. She'd had bosses who were all eyes and who would doubtless have been all hands if they thought they could get away with it. Jared wasn't like that; he was a perfect gentleman. That made Jess's feelings for him all the warmer. It made her fantasies feel innocent and stopped her feeling guilty at harbouring such a colossal crush on another woman's husband.

She felt he enjoyed having her around, too, even if she did prefer the window open while he liked it closed.

The second after he went out, saying, 'I'm just nipping over to the factory,' Jess ran to the sash window and yanked it open.

A couple of seconds later, he was back, having forgotten something. 'It's freezing in here!' he grumbled.

'It's called fresh air,' Jess retorted.

'It's not fresh,' Jared rejoined, 'It's traffic fumes.'

'You two are like husband and wife!' Carl laughed.

Jess turned away to hide her smile, and was pleased to see out of the corner of her eye that Jared was smiling, too.

As much as Jess looked forward to seeing Jared each day, she was glad it wasn't just the two of them cooped up in the office together. In the afternoon, Rudi and Angie came in to do telesales, which basically meant opening a tatty local telephone directory and calling everyone in it, in order.

Rudi was a fun-loving, hyperactive young man, fresh out of drama school but yet to find stardom on the stage. As skinny as a rope, he had a middle eastern appearance but prided himself on being a 'man of a thousand voices'. His primary motive for 'working the phones', as Jared called it, was that he got to try out a different accent every day.

One moment he was a fast-talking, wise-cracking New Yorker, telling the hapless recipients of his calls, 'This will take less time than a cup of caw-fee and save you a whole lotta cash.' The next he was a rural Irishman, passing the time of day in a meadow with, 'So what kind of morning are you having there, m'darlin'?'

It cracked Jess up. It was better than watching the telly.

Jared didn't seem to mind his potential customers being cold-called by 'Sean Connery' one day and 'Al Pacino' the next. 'It's commission only,' he explained to Jess. 'All that matters is that he gets appointments.'

Jess liked it when Jared told her things about the way the business worked. She wasn't particularly interested in salesmanship or double glazing, but she liked the fact that he considered her important enough to explain things to. It gave her a warm feeling that he was somehow taking her under his wing and going out of his way to make her feel included.

Over the years, a lot of people had told Jess she was bright, but she'd always laughed off the notion. She knew she wasn't thick, but she always saw herself as someone who didn't know much about anything. Compared with shining lights like Becky, she considered herself quite naive about most things and could never think of anything she would say she was good at.

On the other hand, Jared gave off an impression of knowing things, and being good at things. When he told her stuff about the business, it didn't feel like he was showing off, or trying to make her feel stupid for not already knowing. It felt like he considered her intelligent enough to understand the things he was telling her.

The other telesales person, Angie, was a nervy bag of bones with such a worn look that she could have been anywhere between thirty and fifty, although Jess guessed she was nearer the former, since her shift ended when she dashed off to collect her daughter from school.

When Angie wasn't outside having a cigarette break — which she seemed to need every other call — she took a market stall approach to selling by phone. 'I could sell water to a drownin' man, me!' Angie cackled, when Jared had introduced her.

At times, Angie's sales calls sounded like she was catching up with a long lost sister and at other times as if she were having a full-blown row. But although Jared raised an eyebrow at one of Angie's more heated exchanges, he said nothing to chasten her.

'Every salesperson is different, because every customer is different,' he explained to Jess, when Angie slammed down her phone and stormed downstairs to cool down. 'On some of the estates she does really well.'

Angie's sporadic gloating successes seemed to bear this out. The first time she secured an appointment in Jess's presence, she sprang from her chair, ran over to Jared's desk and gave the bell a good, loud shake while shouting 'Who's the best? Who's the best?' at the top of her voice.

Jess almost jumped out of her skin and wondered if her frayed nerves would survive the week. At least life at the Brachan Window Company was never dull, she reflected, ruefully.

Throughout the day, and throughout the week, various sales people — the closers — came and went. Sometimes they bounced in, saying, 'Nearly there!' Other times they trudged and muttered, 'Time wasters!' Some stayed a while, making calls and doing paperwork. Others just picked up appointment cards from Jared, then hurried off again.

Among them was Taffy, a red-faced and irascible Welshman who became more red-faced and irascible every time someone called him Taffy, even though everyone did, every time they spoke to him.

'It's a term of affection,' Jared tried to placate him, after Angie deliberately used the word so many times Taffy looked on the brink of thumping her.

'It's not a term of affection,' Taffy grumbled to Jess. 'In Wales, if you call someone Taffy, it's an insult!'

At that moment, Carl stormed into the office and literally threw his briefcase onto his desk. It skidded across the surface and slammed into the wall with a bang. His jacket flew through the air with the snapping sound of a sail in a high wind and landed on the back of his swivel chair with such force that the chair spun around.

'Time wasters?' Jared asked, dryly.

'Nutters, more like!' Carl retorted.

'It's these leads!' he complained. 'Rudi's are okay, Angie's are okay, but some of the leads those door-knockers are bringing back . . . '

'Rough with the smooth, Carl,' Jared said, calmly.

'Why can't I just have the leads Rudi gets?' Carl demanded.

'Because you're not the only sales-man around here!' said Taffy, leaping up from his desk.

'He's right,' Jared said firmly. 'I divide up the leads evenly.'

Carl blew out his anger in a hiss of expelled breath. Turning on his heel, he stalked to the tiny kitchenette. 'Bet there's no tea or milk,' he grumbled.

As abruptly as a change in the wind, Carl's frustration reverted to his more familiar boyish light-heartedness. 'Hang on a minute — not only do we have tea, we've got a choice of Earl Grey, English Breakfast, Darjeeling and green tea. Plus biscuits and fresh milk! And not only that . . . ' his tone changed to one of absolute astonishment, 'Someone has

34

actually cleaned the sink and emptied the bin!'

Jared leaned back behind his desk, basking in reflected glory, and told him, 'Thank our new secretary.'

Carl gave Jess a long look of renewed appreciation. 'Well, hello Mary Poppins! I always said this place needed a woman's touch.'

* * *

'So how's it going with the Hattersleys?' Taffy asked, when Jared popped out to take a call from Suzanne on his mobile.

'Now they are time wasters,' Carl sighed. 'I think they just like having me round for a chat.'

Carl brought his tea over and perched on the side of Jess's desk. She moved her chair back, resenting his casual invasion of her personal space but not yet feeling secure enough in the firm to give his leg a swipe with the back of her hand and tell him to shove off. In any case, a man like Carl would take a woman smacking him on the leg as encouragement.

Folding her arms, she looked up at him. With the extra elevation of the desk, he towered over her and leaned back on the wall like he owned the place. Feeling dowdy in her cheap suit, she found herself getting angry at him for looking so elegant in his expensive shirt, waistcoat and silk tie. She noticed Carl's silver tie-clip was the twin of Jared's.

Carl looked down at her with a regal smile. 'So, Jess, how are you enjoying life at the Brachan Window Company?'

'More like the broken window company,' Taffy muttered.

'The lions' den,' Carl leered.

Jess was tempted to tell him that if he thought he was a lion, he was kidding himself, but she didn't want a row with Carl. For one thing, he was in thick with Jared. They were always shooting the breeze about football, or computer games, or the gadgets Carl had bought for his pride and joy — a BMW the duplicate of Jared's. Carl had more sway with the boss than she did, and she didn't want to lose her job before she'd barely begun it. Also, Carl was mostly out of the office, so tolerating him when he was around wasn't such a big deal.

'It's okay, thanks,' she said, mildly.

In a more conspiratorial way, Carl nodded towards Jared's currently vacant desk and said, 'And how are you getting along with the old man?'

'Fine.' She hoped he didn't hear the slight squeak in her voice.

Carl licked his lips. 'I don't suppose he's told you why his last secretary had to leave?'

She suspected Carl was winding her up, but she was desperately intrigued nonetheless, so she turned to Taffy for further elaboration.

'You must have noticed Jared's missus is a bit . . . well, she's got it in for him,' said the Welshman. 'So, if you put two and two together . . . '

'You mean he had something going

37

on with his secretary?' Jess blurted. Carl laughed at her innocence. He used a hand to describe the curve of a pregnant belly. Jess felt as if a trapdoor had opened beneath her chair. 'You're kidding me!'

'He always employs the pretty ones, doesn't he, Taf?'

'That he does, boyo.'

Jess wished her face wasn't suddenly on fire. 'Well his wife needn't worry about me. He's not my type at all.'

'Really?' Carl looked at her closely. 'So what is your type, Jess?'

This time, Jess was ready to give him a swipe and tell him to shove off her desk. Before she could, they all spun around at the urgent sound of high heels clattering up the wooden stairs. The door banged open so hard, Jess thought it would come off its hinges. Framed in the doorway, filling it with jutting shoulder pads and enormously sculptured hair wrapped in a scarf, stood a power-dressed woman who looked like Sophia Loren working on an

Oscar for Most Wronged And Revengeful Actress In An Over-Acted Latin American Drama.

'Where's Jared?' she demanded. 'I have to see him!'

Her commanding Italian accent even sounded like Sophia Loren. For a moment, Jess was certain it was Jared's wife. Her stomach went queasy. Then she remembered that Suzanne had an English accent.

'I thought he was downstairs, making calls,' said Carl.

Angie pointed at the floor. 'Downstairs placing a bet, more like.'

'Sophia' harrumphed theatrically, turned on a killer heel, and clattered back down the stairs.

'What's the betting somebody hasn't been paid?' Carl muttered.

'Who was that?' Jess asked.

'Lana, Queen of the Jungle,' said Carl.

'Our top closer,' said Taffy.

Carl sprang off the desk and began jumping up and down on the balls of his feet, fists raised, like a sparring boxer. 'Wash your mouth out, Taffy!'

Taffy matched the sparring posture and began bobbing and weaving. 'You couldn't close your sock drawer!' the Welshman taunted.

'Ha!' said Carl, pointing at a whiteboard that dominated one of the office's side walls. 'So who's top of the sales board?'

This was a case of leaping without looking, for Taffy was able to point at the board and shout, 'Nobody! Because there isn't a sale on the board!'

Carl harrumphed then grabbed his jacket. 'Weel, there soon will be. You lot might have time to sit around gossiping all day, but some of us have sales to close!'

When Carl was gone, Jess beckoned Taffy over and hissed, 'Is that true? About the secretary?'

'Ah,' the Welshman smiled mysteriously. 'That's something we may never really know.' But he never expanded on that since, at that moment, Jared returned to the office.

'Are we closing or posing?' he boomed.

'Always closing,' Taffy muttered. 'Lana was looking for you.'

'Good job she didn't find me, then!' Jared grinned, smugly.

'Trouble?' asked Taffy.

'Dispute on her big sale last month. Client claims he was misled. Unfortunately they've taken it up to head office, so it's out of my hands. But the bottom line is, if we don't get paid, she don't get paid.'

3

The week flew by so fast that Jess was startled to find it was Friday afternoon already and the end of her trial period. She was just putting a file on Jared's desk, when he said, 'Take a seat please, Jess.'

His formal tone made her suddenly fearful. The week had been so continually confusing and disorientating she was by no means confident she had lived up to his expectation. She sweated a moment and felt her pulse quickening while she waited for him to finish writing.

The faint beginning of a smile on his lips as he finally looked up, flooded her with relief. He tried to compose his features into something stern and boss-like, but it was too late. She'd already seen what was behind the mask and they both knew it. Smiling herself, she realised, they were getting to know each other.

Nevertheless, he persisted with the stern look as he said, 'Well Jess, you've been here five days, and you've managed to be late every single day.' She tried to make her smile look like a guilty one, but knew she wasn't being any more convincing than he was. 'You've also driven me to drink,' he continued, 'by opening the window every time I shut it.'

Jess glanced towards the back of the office, where they'd eventually reached a compromise. The sash stayed open, but just a little, propped up by an old book. Her smile stopped even pretending to look guilty.

'On the plus side, however,' Jared was openly smiling now, and that smile was doing something so unbelievably silly to her that she hoped he couldn't see how hot and gooey she'd gone, like a piece of melted toffee, from head to toe.

'On the plus side,' Jared repeated — and perhaps he could see how gooey she'd gone, because he'd started to look a little red himself. 'You've worked a miracle with our filing system, you're a faultless typist and you're good on the phone.'

He glanced appreciatively around the office and said, with a slightly embarrassed clearing of his throat, 'I think the flowers on the desks is a very nice touch. So, Jessica Watkins, are you happy to join our team on a permanent basis?'

It was all Jess could do not to fling herself across his desk and kiss him. 'Oh, Jared,' she gushed, 'I mean, Mr King. I'd love to!'

Jared looked pleased, if maybe a tad taken aback, by the warmth of her reaction. Then he said, casually, 'By the way, you can lose those clothes whenever you're ready.'

'What?' she squeaked in horror.

Jess had tried to put from her mind the story of Jared and his last secretary. She'd put him on a pedestal and didn't want to think of him as the kind of man who went around impregnating secretaries. Well, not other secretaries, she'd thought for one minx-ish moment. But having almost convinced herself she'd never even heard the story, it suddenly came back and hit her like a lorry.

Jared looked as flustered as a man who'd accidentally sworn in front of a nun. 'Eh, what I meant to say was I noticed you haven't seemed entirely comfortable in that suit. If you'd rather come to work in jeans and trainers, that's fine by me.'

Jess didn't know what to say. Was he so perceptive he knew what she was happiest wearing — or was he just saying her suit was a mess? The awkward silence was broken by the door banging open. Carl strode across the room. He yanked the bell off Jared's desk and began shaking it wildly.

'Who's the best?' He chanted. 'Who's the best?'

It was last thing Friday afternoon and most of the sales force had straggled into the office for a final debrief on the week's progress. Even Lana, the Queen of the Jungle, was slouched on a swivel chair, looking as mean as a wounded lioness. As the ringing bell shook life into them, all the salespeople — except Lana — rose to their feet, crowded around Carl and began slapping his back and shouting 'You are! You are!'

'The Hattersleys?' Jared beamed.

'The one and only! Listen to this!' Putting down the bell, Carl held up a contract, cleared his throat, and in the manner of a town crier began to read, 'Eight windows, two doors, fascias, gutters, drainpipes and, wait for it, wait for it . . . bargeboards!'

'You beauty!' said Jared. He wasn't addressing Carl, he was addressing the contract, which he ripped from Carl's hands and kissed with a passion that made Jess almost faint.

'Hang about,' said Jared, grabbing Carl's arm. 'Where's the deposit?'

'There.' Carl, pointed at the contract.

'It's supposed to be 20 per cent.' Jared retorted.

'I know, I know. But it was something to do with them having to move some money into a different account. A hundred quid was the biggest cheque they could write at the moment. I know it's a pain. But even so . . . '

'Yes,' said Jared, 'Even so . . . ' And suddenly, he was beaming again. 'This deserves a celebration. Last one in the pub buys the whole evening!'

Almost before he'd finished speaking, the others were pulling on their jackets, with Carl and Taffy racing to be first through the door. It was then that Jess, as Jared's secretary, remembered a call she'd taken earlier.

'Don't forget it's your son's parent evening.'

Jared's eyes met hers and, for a fleeting moment, he looked so torn and guilty that she hurt for him. At last, he said, 'I've got time for a couple of drinks first. Will you join us, Jess?'

The question was asked so casually, with such an easy smile, and with such a nice look in his eyes that Jess wasn't sure whether she could hear her heart pounding or whether it was just the sound of the last salesmen rumbling down the stairs. Embarrassed, she gestured at the now empty and silent salesroom and said with a grin, 'We'll be the last ones there and have to buy all the drinks.'

'Don't worry,' he smiled, 'I was going to treat them all anyway.'

Like a man with all the time in the world, he picked his jacket from his chair and put it on. Then he picked up Jess's coat and held it open for her, so that she could slip her arms in.

It was an innocent gesture on his part, she knew that. But she held her breath as she turned her back on him, straightened her spine and put her arms back. She closed her eyes as he drew the garment up her arms and brought the collar together around her shoulders. His fingers didn't even brush her, but with her eyes closed the feel of the coat settling around her felt like a hug.

★ ★ ★

Boy, it felt funny walking down the high street with Jared King. By the time he'd closed the window, turned off the lights and locked up, the others were long gone, so they were completely alone among the coming and going commuters and shoppers. It didn't feel like boss and employee, just a man and a woman walking down the street, him looking rich and authoritative in his well-cut suit, her feeling a bit self-conscious about being with the best turned-out man in town.

After that deliciously intimate moment when he'd draped her coat around her, it almost felt like a date. Not that there was anything illicit about what they were doing, she reminded herself. They were going to a very public place to be part of a group of workers celebrating a colleague's success. What could be more above board? Especially since he was married.

And yet . . . they weren't part of the

office group at the moment. The high street felt like a strangely neutral territory, neither work nor social, a place outside of their usual lives, where different rules and possibilities applied.

She wondered if Jared felt the same way about this strange transitional space where, for a moment at least, he had to face neither the responsibility of a busy office nor the pressure of what she had become convinced was a troubled and painful marriage.

He hadn't spoken to her since he'd slipped her coat on her shoulders, so she was entirely alone with her fevered thoughts. Was it her imagination or was he walking particularly slowly, dragging out the moment? Was it just the freedom he was enjoying or was he enjoying sharing that moment with her?

What was that little smile he'd given her, when he'd pulled the book out of the sash window before he closed it? Well, she knew it was just about their little running battle of him shutting the window, her opening the window. It had become their little joke, but there was something special about sharing secret smiles over 'their' joke.

They reached the pub and he held the door open. It was a big, dark, noisy pub, jam-packed with Friday after-workers. He put his hand lightly between her shoulder blades as he guided her through the crowd. It was an unconscious gesture, to stop her getting jostled, and he didn't even glance down at her. But she felt his palm burning through her coat, and the warmth of his body, brushing against her side, in the hot intimacy of the inky crush.

The sales force had colonised a corner alcove and Taffy hailed them as they approached: 'Here they come at last!'

Taffy's 'they' while Jared's hand was still on her back, struck Jess like a dart. It was like they were a couple, arriving together.

'We're dying of thirst here, boss!' Carl shouted.

Jared took out his wallet with an easy smile, and thumbed out a credit card. 'What are we all having then? Come on, we might as well eat as well.'

The team instantly began squabbling over a couple of menus. Jared stood there, tall and calm, nodding slightly to acknowledge each request they called to him.

Jess stood beside him, watching him, and she didn't think she had ever seen a man look so rich or completely at home at the top of a hierarchy. In that moment, he wasn't just a boss, or even a leader, he really was a king, dispensing favours on his subjects as if the fact he was about to drop a few hundred quid was nothing to him. Jess had never stood beside such a man before, and she couldn't help but feel a thrill by association.

As they'd arrived last, Jared and Jess found themselves squeezed up together in the space that opened for them around the large circular table.

As the empty bottles, glasses and

used plates piled up, and the voices grew louder, the talk was mainly past adventures and exploits in the macho world of salesmanship. Lana, dressed in a dazzling yellow trouser suit, was every bit as competitive and boastful as the boys.

It wasn't a subject Jess could contribute to and it didn't particularly interest her. But sitting so close to Jared, their hips touching on the banquette seating was exciting enough.

It was utter fantasy, of course. There was no way she would ever get involved with a married man, even if he did make the slightest move in her direction, which of course he hadn't. But when there was nothing else happening in that area of your life, what was wrong with a little fantasy to keep your blood warm? She bet that was how a lot of people got through the working day. As a vodka and tonic began to hit her, she wondered what Jared fantasised about. She hoped nobody noticed her stifled giggle.

Jared was in a quiet, self-contained mood, content to let the others do the talking, and Carl was eager as ever to show off, especially as the booze began to redden his pale features.

'You know what I like bes', Jess?' Carl said, pointing at her, with a slightly swaying hand that also held a glass of red wine. Jess didn't want to know, but Carl told her anyway. 'The thing I like bes', Jess, is when you go into the front room and they've got the telly on.' Carl glanced around the table with an *Am I right?* look on his face. 'Do you know what you do then, Jess?' Carl asked. 'You go straight up to the telly and you turn it off.'

'That's right, boyo,' Taffy muttered.

'At that moment, Jess, you can hear a pin drop. It's like that saloon bar scene in a western when the music stops and everyone looks at the gunslinger. And it's at that moment when you know if you're gonna walk out with a cheque. Because if none of them challenge you for switching off their telly, they've accepted that you're the boss.'

Jared rewarded Carl with an indulgent grin and although Jess could see he was patronising him, the blond man basked in it.

'Talking of tellies!' Taffy jumped in excitedly. 'There was this guy at my last firm. He used to get his window sample out in their front room, hold it like this, see, and give it a good kick with his shoe to show them how tough the glass was. One day he booted it so bloomin' hard he booted it right out of his hands and it went straight through their telly!'

As the stories went on and the laughter got louder, Jess felt a knot of worry tightening in her stomach. Jared was supposed to be at his son's parents' evening. She wondered if he had forgotten, and whether or not she should remind him?

At that moment, though, Jared was leaning out of the group towards a waiter. 'Same again, everyone?'

'Nothing for me,' said Jess.

'You sure?'

'Just water, then.' She wasn't really a drinker and in her nervousness she'd already had too much, too quickly. Everything had taken on a soft, woozy edge, and she was glad she was sitting down, wedged in tightly between Jared and Lana. Her only hope was that if she stopped now, she would sober up enough not to be wobbly when she eventually stood up.

Jared blinked at her, and shrugged. Everyone else was knocking back the hard stuff like sailors on shore leave, no one more so than Lana. As they grew more raucous and befuddled, they seemed to notice less and less that Jess was mentally slipping away and into a little bubble of her own.

Even Jared seemed to have forgotten she was there. He was turned away from her, engaged with Taffy in a heated argument about which Jess had not a clue. On her other side, Lana was getting more and more flamboyantly forceful and Italian as she locked horns with Carl over something that, again, was completely lost on Jess.

So much for romantic fantasies, thought Jess. As she stared with increasing resentment at Jared's back, she realised that she really didn't know him at all. Sometimes, when they were alone, she thought he was completely different from the other salesmen, with their boorish machismo, one-upmanship and the underhand sales techniques in which they took such pride, but when he was with them, she couldn't tell them apart.

Look at him now; not just ignoring her, but shamelessly ignoring his responsibilities as a husband and father. How was his wife going to feel when he didn't show up at the parents' evening? How was his boy going to feel? She felt guilty for still not reminding him. But then she thought, to heck with him. He knew what he was doing and he deserved what he got.

Becoming bored, Jess wished she wasn't so tightly boxed in behind the table. It would be hard to get up and go home without a fuss. Stealing a look at her watch, she saw it was getting on for eleven.

It was at that moment that the party was silenced by an ear-splitting female shriek. The whole pub seemed to shut up and listen. Even the music and the jangling of the slot machines seemed to fade into silence. It was that pin-drop moment Carl had spoken of, when someone turns off the telly, everyone looks round, and you suddenly find out who's in charge.

'Jared!' The woman screamed. 'What do you think you're doing?'

Jared turned away from Taffy and sat up, in drunken slow motion. At the far side of the table stood the angriest redhead Jess had ever seen.

'Do you know,' she spat, 'how embarrassing it was for me to be there on my own tonight? As if there aren't already enough rumours about our so-called marriage!'

Jared tried to form his lips into a smirk, but in Jess's eyes it just made him look more drunk and stupid. He cast a slow, sluggish glance around the table, as if trying to gather support from his staff. It was like he was trying to say, *Look at her. You see what I have to put up with?* But there was no support forthcoming. Eyes were averted, heads turned away. It was like everyone was trying to sink into their seats and hope they weren't noticed.

And so Jared just sat there, like a punch-drunk boxer on the ropes, saying nothing, while his wife let him have it. It took a while, for there was a lot to come — several years of a disintegrating marriage, hurled across the table in words like spears, while it seemed as if every last person in the pub stood there watching and listening agog, as if it was a scene from a soap opera being played out on the big screen above the bar.

Eventually, it seemed that Suzanne had vented herself of every shred of hatred, bitterness and contempt. For a long moment she stood there, breathing hard, red eyed, trembling slightly, literally exhausted.

Then she pointed at Jared and threw her final spear. 'Don't even think of trying to get in my front door tonight!'

4

On Monday, because she dreaded what she would find, Jess was even later than usual. As she bounced up the stairs in her scuffed trainers, the bell was already ringing. As she reached the door at the top, she found herself swimming against a tide of unfamiliar faces coming the other way.

When she'd finally untangled herself from the new crop of canvassers leaving the building, she was surprised to see that the man behind the desk with the bell in his hand was Carl.

'Where's Jared?' she asked.

Carl made a pantomime of consulting his watch. 'And what time do you call this, Miss Watkins?'

'Time someone told you you're not remotely funny,' said Jess. Jared had been right about that cheap suit. She felt a lot more confident in her more usual clothes.

As she hung up her coat, Carl feigned even greater horror, observing, 'Jeans, Miss Watkins?'

'Give it up,' said Jess, as she opened the window. 'Jared said I could wear them. Where is he, anyway?'

'Head office. There was a message for him first thing. PG Brachan himself, no less.'

'Is it about Lana's dispute?'

Carl shrugged. 'Who knows, who cares? But I do know he left me in charge, so you can wait on me, for a change. Tea with milk, no sugar, since you ask. Hurry now, boss is waiting.'

He gave her such a pearly grin that Jess could only roll her eyes. But she made his tea, and one for herself, because she wanted to find out what had happened. As she carried the mugs from the kitchenette — she gave him the one emblazoned with 'Duh!' — Carl was leaning back in Jared's chair, his hands behind his head and his highly polished brogues up on the desk.

'You really want to be him, don't

you?' Jess observed, as she sat down across the desk from him. 'Look at you; same shirt, same shoes. You're even wearing the same signet ring.'

Carl swung his feet off the desk. 'What you wear is very important in this business. Take you, Jess. I'm not being nasty, but that getup's alright in here, where nobody sees you, but . . . '

'Thanks a lot!'

'But suppose you went into the house of a high-earning client dressed like that? He'd think you made the teas in a hairdressers or something. So why would he trust you with a twenty thousand pound contract? Whereas I pull up in the Beamer, he sees the Saville Row suit, the briefcase from Harrods . . . Success equals competence, Jess. So he gives me the order. It's the three Is — image, image, image.'

'See what I mean?' said Jess. 'You even copy his lines.'

Carl snorted, then said, pointedly, 'Well I wouldn't want to be him today.'

On that, they were in agreement. Suzanne's tirade still vivid in her mind, Jess felt a wave of deep sympathy for him, followed by an even deeper wave of guilt. When Suzanne was laying into him, and his so-called friends were pretending they were somewhere else, Jess was as bad as the rest.

Her behaviour later was even more cowardly.

When Suzanne stormed out, the pub looked like the aftermath of a terrorist attack. Even the people who weren't in their party looked shell-shocked. Carl said, 'Forget her. Drink up.' But there was little support for the idea. Taffy muttered, 'Let's call it a night.'

Jess didn't even say goodbye. She mumbled about going to the loo and as soon as she was out of sight, walked straight out of the pub.

As the cold night air hit her, her eye-make-up streaked down her cheeks at the awfulness of what had happened. She felt every bit of the pain Suzanne had hurled at him. She hated herself for deserting him, but she knew the alternative could only end in disaster. The fair-weather drinking pals shoving off, abandoning him. The loyal secretary sticking around to help. Him looking at her, with nowhere else to go . . .

Her body burned for him, but she didn't want it in those circumstances, with the black rain cloud of a regretful morning after hanging over her. The sullied picture of them unable to look at each other turned her stomach. She wanted the stained glass windows, the church bells and the wedding cake dress. If anything was going to happen between her and Jared, she wanted him to hear the trumpets, too. That didn't stop her feeling his pain, though.

'Where did he go in the end?' she asked.

'Crashed out at my place, didn't he? Taffy's got a wife and kids, so he couldn't go there. I think Lana would have taken him in,' Carl smirked. 'But even Jared has to draw the line somewhere.'

Jess felt a fierce stab of jealousy at the thought of the dominant and predatory Lana, closing in on Jared, with hot Italian passion on her mind. She was relieved when Carl said, 'Besides, Lana's got this torrid on-off thing going on with a hot-blooded Hungarian ballet dancer. Get caught between those two and you'd probably wind up dead.'

'Did Suzanne let him back in, in the end?' Jess asked.

'You've got to be kidding. He's had it coming a long time and this time there's no going back. We spent all Saturday just trying to get her to let him pick up some of his stuff because all he had was what he stood up in. Eventually — and I mean eventually — she agreed that I could go round and get it for him. She didn't even open the door. She'd just dumped it all in a heap at the end of the drive.'

'How awful!'

'You can say that again. You should

see the whacking great house he lived in. Palace of a place, up on Elm Road. Well, he won't be seeing the inside of that place again.'

'Is he still staying with you?'

'I'm not a hostel,' Carl said, indignantly.

'So where's he living?'

'Have a spy with your little eye,' Carl grinned. He nodded at a couple of suits in dry-cleaner's bags, draped over Jared's filing cabinet. In the corner behind it was a rolled-up sleeping bag, a suitcase, a sports bag and a pile of well stuffed bin liners that apparently held everything that Jared had left to show for his years on the planet.

'He's sleeping in the office?' Jess's heart broke for him. 'The poor man.'

'Spare me the violins!' Carl sneered. 'It's better than a park bench. Anyway, if you're so concerned, why don't you offer him a bed?'

'Grow up, Carl!' Jess glared at him.

It was the first time she and Carl had been alone together. Usually, everything he said was a means of showing off in front of Jared or Taffy. It was like talking to a man who constantly had one eye in the mirror to check how handsome and clever he looked. Without an audience to play to, she'd hoped he'd be less of an idiot. She felt like shaking him and saying, *Nobody's watching, nobody's impressed. Just be yourself.*

He was observant, though, always trying to spot ways of reading his clients' minds, she supposed. Right now, he was watching her closely. 'Why are you so concerned about him, anyway?'

'More to the point,' Jess retorted sharply, 'Why are you so unconcerned? I thought you were his friend.'

Carl curled his lip at the word. 'He's only my boss, Jess.'

Jess looked at him incredulously. 'But what about all the hanging around you do together? All the chat about cars and football? All that copying everything he wears, for that matter. Doesn't it go any deeper with you two? Don't you care about what's happened to him? When someone's marriage breaks up, it's not just a big joke, you know.'

Carl crossed his arms, defensively. 'Do you think he'd find it any less funny if it was me in his shoes?'

'Yes, I do,' said Jess. 'You might be too thick-skinned to notice, but Jared cares a lot. He cares about all of his staff. He's a nice guy, Carl.'

Carl squirmed uncomfortably. Then he leaned forward on the desk. His smug mask slipping for once, he looked a little raw. 'Don't forget I've spent half the weekend babysitting him. I can't be that bad, can I?'

Jess saw the silent plea in his baby blue eyes for her not to think quite so badly of him and she felt some of her annoyance melting. No, she reconsidered, I suppose you're not that bad, deep down.

Carl, however, had clearly had enough soul bearing for one day. He stood up as if he needed to strut about a bit to get back to his arrogant self.

'You might think I copy Jared, but there's one big difference. I'm on the way up and he's finished. Worse, he can't even see it. That's why I don't have much sympathy for him.'

Jess was so indignant on Jared's behalf she was lost for words. But Carl was building up a head of steam.

'It's not just his marriage that's failed. He may have been a hot shot once, but he lost it years ago. Look at this place! No wonder they call it the broken window company. It's falling apart around him.'

'You work here, too!' Jess retorted.

'Not for much longer.'

For a second, Carl looked caught out, as if he he'd let slip a secret. But then, having started, he couldn't stop himself going on. As he did, she saw him transforming before her eyes; the sneering arrogance giving way to the excitement of a kid at Christmas.

'Golden Windows have offered me a job. You've seen their flashy new showroom at the other end of the high street, haven't you? They want me to run it. You should see the package they're giving me. Ten salesmen under me — and a Porsche!'

He looked as if he'd been dreaming of this moment all his life and there was such a boyish innocence about him that Jess couldn't help forgetting some of his nastiness moments before. Under it all, he was just a big kid dying to be liked.

'I'm glad for you,' said Jess, and realised she actually was.

What he said next, though, took her by surprise. 'The new office needs a secretary. I'm doing the hiring and firing. How d'you fancy coming with me?'

'What, you'd hire someone who looks like they make tea in a hairdressers?' she retorted.

'Obviously we'd have to get you some new threads . . . ' he grinned. He sized her up. 'Prada, I'd say. It's a reception role; frontline desk as they come in the door. It needs someone gorgeous. That's why I thought of you.'

Jess laughed gently. 'You're not top salesman for nothing, are you?'

'I mean it,' he said, levelly. Jess blushed and looked away. 'So can I take that a yes, then?'

'I've already got a job.'

'The pay's better than you get here. Plus everything's new and shiny; new computer, new desk with a nice leather top, thick carpet under your feet. I'll even swing you a couple of Prada suits as office expenses.'

Jess glanced at the threadbare orange rugs they were standing on and the battered desks with their yellowing phones, her ancient computer. Her faded jeans and her scuffed trainers, for that matter.

'What is there to keep you in this dump?' Carl pressed her. And as much as she wanted to resist his hard-sell she had to admit he had a point. What was there to keep her here?

Except Jared, of course. Becky would tell her she was living on dreams again, while reality knocked on her forehead and wondered if she was home. But she felt strongly protective of Jared. She wasn't about to desert him in his hour of need, and while she couldn't blame Carl for following his own dream, the departure of Jared's top salesman was going to be an extra blow to him at a time when he had enough to cope with.

'Does he know you're leaving?' she asked.

Carl looked guilty. 'I've been waiting for the right moment to tell him. But since what happened on Friday . . .'

Jess understood Carl's dilemma. But keeping the news from Jared would be even worse. 'You've got to tell him. It's only fair.'

Carl nodded. 'I will, I will. Just let me find the right moment, okay?' He looked suddenly fearful. 'You won't say anything, will you?'

The burden of keeping a secret from Jared was the last thing Jess needed. But she could hardly betray Carl's confidence. 'Just don't leave it too long,' she said, sharply.

'So what about the reception job?' Carl asked.

'I'll think about it.' At that moment, the phone beeped. Jess answered, then pressed the mute button. 'It's Mr Hattersley for you.'

Carl went white. 'Tell him he's just missed me.' Then, in a slightly panicky voice, 'Find out what he wants.'

Jess went back to the phone. A few minutes later, she told Carl, 'He's having second thoughts about the order. He said to tell you he knows his rights; that he's entitled to a fourteen-day cooling off period because he signed the contract in his own home. Is that true?'

Carl bunched his fists and glared at the ceiling. 'I knew this would happen!' He grabbed his coat and briefcase. 'Not a word to Jared about this until I get back. I'll going over to the Hattersleys now and try to turn this thing around.'

Jess watched him go, and wondered how she'd ended up conspiring with him. Just whose side was she supposed to be on?

* * *

Jess was alone in the office when Jared's heavy footsteps came trudging up the stairs. She heard the sigh and knew it was him before he even opened the door. He looked awful; exhausted from three nights of broken sleep on sofas and floors, not to mention what he must be feeling inside.

Jess felt like hugging him, but with a man like Jared, you just didn't. Regardless of his red eyes and dark shadows, he still carried himself like the master of his kingdom. He didn't look like the sort of man who'd collapse sobbing into anyone's bosom. He gave the impression that if you tried to comfort him he'd look at you as if you'd gone mad.

He glanced at the desks where Rudi and Angie were normally on the phone. 'Where is everyone?'

Glad to talk business, Jess said, 'Rudi's gone for an audition, and Angie said her little girl's off school with a cold.'

'What's the audition for?' Jared asked.

'Chorus in The Lion King.'

Jared raised his eyebrows and smiled. 'Fingers crossed, then. Anything else happening?'

Jess thought about Carl's new job, and the snag with the Hattersley deal, but instead she asked him, 'Would you like a cup of tea?'

'Thanks.'

Glad to get away, Jess hurried towards the kitchenette and froze, mid-stride, as Jared said cheerily, 'That's a lovely top, Jess.'

Completely motionless, she barely dared peak over her shoulder to check that he'd actually said that. He immediately sounded embarrassed. 'Sorry to be personal. I just think you look a lot more comfortable in casual clothes and that colour really suits you.'

'Thanks,' Jess squeaked as she ran into the kitchenette and, as tiny as it was, wondered how long she could hide in there.

It was the first personal compliment he had paid her. Her nerve endings were firing like electric shocks and her heart was beating like a bass drum. Eventually, when she could hide no more, she carried two mugs to Jared's desk, trying for all she was worth not to spill them.

Jared didn't look up from his paperwork. She put his tea on the desk, but didn't sit down opposite, as she had with Carl. With Jared, it wasn't her place to, unless invited. So she lingered, mug in her hand.

She couldn't leave Friday's events uncommented on. She couldn't leave her sympathy unexpressed. But suddenly she had no idea how to broach the subject. Foolishly, she'd assumed he might bring it up; an assumption on her part that conveniently ignored the fact she'd never once heard him talk about his private life.

'Did you sort out Lana's dispute?' she asked.

'Huh?'

'At head office, this morning.'

He looked up, puzzled. He made a non-committal sound and went back to his paperwork.

Jess sucked her teeth. Then, gathering all her courage, decided she'd just have to go for it. 'Are you . . . okay?' she asked gently.

Again, he looked puzzled. For a moment she thought she was going to have to write it on the bloomin' blackboard for him. Eventually she saw him get her drift.

'I'm fine,' he said flatly. In fact, he almost looked it.

'Really?' she pressed.

He looked cornered, as Carl had earlier, and Jess wondered what you had to do to make these men acknowledge their emotions. Realising she'd have to do all the work, she said, 'I think what happened was so awful . . . '

Jared followed her glance towards his rolled up sleeping bag and other displaced possessions. He shifted, uneasily. 'Look, Jess, don't go all mother hen on me. I'm a big boy and this is a temporary situation. It's just for a couple of days until I can get a flat sorted out. I'm fine, okay?'

The edge in his voice sliced her. *Sorry I asked*, she thought bitterly, as she felt the faintest of pricking in the corners of her eyes.

He seemed to see it and his face tinged with guilt. 'Sorry Jess. I appreciate your concern, but I don't need any sympathy. Have a seat.'

She sat down, gratefully. He was clearly uncomfortable discussing his private life and she appreciated the effort he was making for her.

'What happened with Suzanne isn't anything new. We've been living apart in the same house for a long time. Separate rooms, separate lives. The only reason I haven't moved out before now is . . . well, it's complicated.'

'Your son?'

'That's the main reason, yes.'

That rather too casual 'main reason' made Jess wonder if another reason was simply his reluctance to give up the big house Carl had described. She felt unkind for thinking that about him, but with people like Carl and Jared, the cars, the suits, the whole flash image, meant a lot. They weren't merely possessions, they were the way they defined themselves and their place in the pecking order. It wasn't their fault, she decided. It was just the culture they lived in.

'How old is he?' she asked.

'Eight.' Suddenly, he looked all proud dad and Jess was pleased to see the warmth coming back into his eyes. She instinctively scanned his desk for a photo of the boy and realised there were no personal items on display at all. That macho culture again, she thought, never show a sign of softness.

Jared must have realised what she was looking for and he pulled out his wallet, took out a snap shot and handed it over.

'He's gorgeous!' she exclaimed.

'Just like his dad, eh?'

Jess blushed, although she knew it was just a line, fired off like a reflex. But the boy was the spitting image of his father; the eyes, the smile; the faces of Jared and his son seemed to blur and alternate before her eyes, as if the boy was the child Jared had been and Jared was the man the boy would grow up to be. It was like an optical illusion and when she glanced up at him the faces kept on alternating. For all the suits and sales talk, he was still the boy in the picture.

'He's lovely,' she reiterated, as she handed the picture back.

Jared tucked the picture and wallet away again. 'Actually, Jess, there's something I've got to tell you.' Jess was all ears. But Jared was back in business mood. 'This is strictly between you and me, Jess. I'm not going to tell anyone else — yet — but you deserve to know.'

His face told her it was bad news before he said it. 'The meeting at head office wasn't about Lana. It was about this office. They're closing us down.'

5

If Jess had been standing up, her legs would have collapsed beneath her; she actually felt them go numb at the thought of Jared being ripped out of her life. The news was such a shock to her system that for a moment she could see Jared's lips moving but was barely hearing what he said.

' ... sales have been down too long ... it's not just us, but we are next on the list ... '

Jess shook her head to try to clear it. This was an emergency and she had to concentrate.

'Carl will be alright,' Jared was saying. 'Rudi and Angie are only part time. Who knows, he may even win that audition. It's Taffy I feel sorry for. He's the same age as me with a wife, kids, mortgage ... where's he gonna get another job?'

'What about you?' Jess cut in.

'I'll be alright.'

'They'll move you to another office or something?'

Jared gave her a humourless smile. 'They're closing offices, not opening them. If there is another job, it won't be manager. There'll be no basic, no car. Just commission only, out there chasing leads with all the young hot shots like Carl.' Jared sighed, and suddenly looked his age. 'To be honest, Jess, I really don't think I could go back to that.'

'What will you do?'

'Something will turn up.'

His confident smile came as readily as ever, but Jess felt empty, not least because she didn't buy that brave face for a minute. 'It's definite, then?'

'Good as,' said Jared. 'I've got until the end of the month to turn things around, but the chances of that happening . . . ' He gestured at the sales board. Its virgin surface told its own story, but Jess suddenly refused to hear its hopeless message.

'But there is a chance?' she pressed. 'If you can get the sales up they'll keep the office open?'

'In theory . . . '

'Then why are you giving up?' Jess demanded. 'What happened to all that, 'We're the best! We're the best!' stuff?'

Jared gave her a shy smile. 'You sound like you believe it, Jess.'

'Don't you?' she challenged.

For a long steady moment, he held her gaze and all the while she saw a glimmer of life creeping back into his tired face, as if he were drawing energy from her. It was a satisfying feeling for her, like he had a need that she fulfilled or that they were two parts that fitted together to make something bigger.

At last he said, 'We can but try. After all, we've already got Carl's big order from the Hattersleys.'

Jess felt a pang of guilt but it was hardly the moment to tell him that deal looked like it was falling through — or that his top closer was leaving.

Just as she was feeling the pressure of keeping Carl's secret, Jared said, 'You can't tell anyone about this. If they think PG's even thinking about closing us they'll give up and we won't sell anything. I'll have to think of another way to motivate them.'

For a moment he was deep in thought, chin cupped in his big hand. 'I'll have to get out there myself,' he said quietly, more to himself than her. 'Show them how to close a deal or two . . . Got it!' he beamed. 'I'll put my name back on the sales board. Make it a race. If any of them matches my sales by the end of the month, I'll give them my commission, too! Then I'll really steam it — give it the old Jared King special!'

Jess's spirits soared on a flood tide of renewed pride in Jared.

The phone beeped and Jared snatched it up. 'Brachan Window Company.' He listened, then raised his eyebrows at Jess as he said, 'Certainly, sir. Let me just have a look in the diary . . . ' There wasn't a diary on his desk. Instead he picked up a pen and reached for a lead card.

Jess thrilled to his audacity as he winked at her and said, 'The appointment book's actually very full, sir, because of a really special offer that ends tomorrow, but I can squeeze you in at five tonight or seven tomorrow. Which would you prefer?' He wrote down an address and a few notes, then said, 'Tomorrow at seven, then.'

'Good news?' Jess asked with mock innocence.

Jared grinned at her. 'You must be my lucky charm. It seems somebody out there actually wants to buy some windows.'

★　★　★

'Right, men!' said Jared. 'And Lana,' he added. 'There's a new name on the sales board. It's Jared King, spelt, T-O-P-C-L-O-S-E-R.'

Jess couldn't help smiling as Jared

went into his motivational talk. As always, she found it so over the top, but at the same time, she swelled with pride, because he was so good at it. By turns, it was like watching a politician on the campaign trail, an evangelical preacher, a union activist on a soapbox, or Mohamed Ali boasting for the TV cameras. She doubted that even Rudi, with the best script in the world, could put on such a rousing performance. He was so compelling, in fact, that she almost forgot to get the cotton wool in her ears before he got to the bell-ringing.

As Carl and the others prepared to head out, the buoyant mood was shattered when Jess answered the phone to the angriest customer she had ever encountered. As she repeatedly tried to get half a word in edgeways, she was aware of Jared and Taffy hovering around her, alerted to the fact that something very bad was happening.

They could probably hear the man's

anger from several feet away, although he was so incoherent with rage that it took Jess several attempts to calm him down enough to articulate what was actually wrong. When he did, she couldn't blame him for being furious. She told him so, but doubted he heard her, for he was still raging on. It took her another three goes, fighting against the tirade, before she got him to tell her his address. She repeated it aloud as she wrote it down.

As she spoke, Jared snatched open the filing cabinet and, because Jess had organised the filling so well, pulled the file first time.

'I'm just going to put you on hold while I check the file,' Jess told the customer. Breathlessly, she filled Jared in. 'He ordered white windows and they've delivered brown. Unfortunately, they've already fitted two of them and have ripped out another of his old windows before he noticed what they'd done.'

'It's one of Carl's,' Jared muttered, as

he rapidly scanned the contract. 'Customer's right about the white. So is this our fault or is it . . . ' He flipped through the internal paperwork which, again, Jess had arranged in perfect order. He punched the air. 'We're in the clear. It's the factory's fault!'

'What do I tell him?' asked Jess.

'Apologise profusely and tell him we'll change them. Tell him to let the fitters put the brown window in for now and we'll fast track new white windows to him by the end of the week. Tell him we'll knock off the price of one window for his trouble — one and a half if you really have to. I'll get the cost back from the factory.'

He must have noticed how shaken Jess looked, for he added, 'Shall I talk to him?'

'No, I'm okay.' Jess took a deep breath and snatched up the phone. It took her a long time to placate the man, but by the time she eventually returned the phone to its cradle, she was smiling and they parted on good terms. She hadn't even had to discount him a window.

'That was magnificent,' Jared congratulated her.

'I'll make you a cup of tea,' said Taffy, adding, 'I think we could all use one after that.'

'You really handled that well,' Jared reiterated.

'I couldn't have done it without your back-up,' said Jess.

'And I couldn't have given you the back-up if you hadn't done such a great job with the filing. So the credit's all yours, Jess.'

She basked in his undisguised approval.

As Taffy brought the teas over, Jess asked Jared, 'So what was that about our fault or the factory's fault?'

'Brachan doesn't actually make the windows,' Jared explained. 'We sell them and fit them but we buy the frames and glass from an outside supplier. There are two or three good ones we could use. Unfortunately, there's also a cheap one. So guess which one PG Brachan has switched to? I'll call in and sort it out on the way to my meeting.'

★   ★   ★

Angie was still off work with her daughter, but Jess recognised the sound of Rudi's trainers bounding up the stairs at his usual time after lunch.

'How was the audition?' Jess asked.

'Some you win,' he shrugged. It was a line all the closers used, but none of them ever dared to utter the part they actually meant: Some you lose.

'There'll be another one,' Jess sympathised.

'Every no brings you one step nearer to a yes,' said Rudi, in a perfect imitation of Jared. 'Where is the boss man, anyway?'

'Meeting,' said Jess as Rudi opened a phone book.

The meeting was with a divorce lawyer. But he'd entrusted Jess with that information because she was his secretary. She wasn't about to spread gossip of his private affairs to anyone else.

As Rudi began making calls, however, and Jess turned back to her computer, she found it hard to concentrate. Her mind was with Jared, in a solicitor's office, somewhere. She pictured him perched in front of a desk, looking tired, beaten and worried. She could see the papers spread out on the desktop, the lawyer's vaguely pitying expression.

It was like trying to work while a friend had an operation or sat an exam. It couldn't be done, you were just waiting anxiously to see them and find out if it had all gone okay.

She wondered if one day they'd be able to face all of life's crises side by side, not as boss and secretary but as man and — but she hardly dared project her fantasies that far ahead. If Jared's marriage was really over, what had been an impossible dream was suddenly tantalisingly feasible. But so was the fear that he'd never feel that way about her.

★ ★ ★

'Well, I'll be off then,' Rudi said at his usual time.

'See you tomorrow,' said Jess after the longest few hours of her life. As the echo of his trainers bounced away down the stairs, she looked around the empty office. It was her knocking off time, too. Jared had given her a key to lock up, but instead, she hung around and did some listless tidying up, waiting for him to come back.

She just wanted to see him and know that he was alright. She could have phoned and asked how he'd got on, but that felt too pushy, so she hung around in the hope of 'just bumping into him'.

She'd expected him back earlier, and after a while began to wonder if he was coming back at all. He may have gone straight on to his seven o'clock sales appointment. He wouldn't phone and tell her, because he wouldn't expect her to be there.

Eventually, she decided if she stayed any longer it would be too obvious that she'd waited in for him. She was just about to close the window when she heard his footsteps on the stairs.

He came in, whistling softly to himself, then stopped in surprise. 'I'd thought you'd be long gone.'

'I was just going,' said Jess, slightly embarrassed.

In the crook of one arm he cradled a newspaper, three supermarket sandwiches, several packets of crisps and pastries. Bachelor shopping, thought Jess. He must have noticed her looking, and said, 'Want a sandwich since you're still here?'

Now he mentioned it, she realised she was starving. 'I'll put the kettle on,' she grinned.

It was such a domestic scene as they sat at Jared's desk eating sandwiches and crisps — like she was the wife and he'd just come home from work — that

Jess found herself slipping into the role.

'So how did it go?' she asked, as if they always talked so intimately.

Jared waited until he'd finished chewing, then said, 'I'm going to make it easy for her. She can have whatever she wants. All I'm interested in is getting good access to Josh. He's the only good thing that came out of that marriage anyway.'

Jess sipped her tea. 'It must have been good between you once.'

Jared shrugged non-committally while he chewed. Eventually, he said, 'You know what, Jess? It sounds strange, but I'm glad it's all turned out like this. It just feels like such a relief. Even kipping here in the office. It's better than the way we were living this past year.'

Jess nodded, but before she could think of a reply, Jared was looking at his watch. 'Well, I'd better get selling.' He started to clear away the empty food wrapping.

'Let me do that,' said Jess and she leapt up and began tidying while he protested that he could manage. She couldn't help recalling Carl's words about the war of the window: *You're like husband and wife, you two.*

Jared opened his briefcase and checked the contents. 'Been a while since I did this.' He looked almost nervous, which was something she'd never seen in him before, but within minutes the excitement took over. 'Feels like old times.'

Jess handed him a tissue and pointed to the corner of her mouth to indicate that he had some mayo to wipe from his.

'Thanks.' He closed his case. 'Why don't you come with me?'

'Me?' she squeaked.

'You might bring me luck.'

'Okay, then.'

He went to the light switch, then hesitated. 'You'd better put your suit on. We've just got time to stop at your place on the way.'

6

The off-white leather of the BMW's passenger seat was firm and deeply textured, contoured in so many places it hugged her snugly at the hips and shoulders. The big door closed with a soft sound and the engine was barely audible as Jared eased the sleek, black saloon out of the yard and into the cobbled alley at the back. As he turned into the road and pulled away, she felt the effortless power pressing her back into the seat, although the engine note rose to no more than a purr.

Jess glanced at her reflection in the polished walnut of the dashboard and understood why the cars and suits meant so much to Jared and Carl. It wasn't just the image, she realised — the sheer luxury was utterly seductive.

Jared pulled into the kerb in her road

and she was relieved when he said, 'I'll wait here.' She only had a room.

Hurrying up the shared stairs, she let herself in, went to the wardrobe and reached for her charcoal suit. Despite being in a hurry, she hesitated. After the opulence of the BMW, it looked so cheap. But it was the only formal wear she had. She bit her lip as Carl's words floated back into her head. *You look like you make the teas in a hairdressers . . . it's the three Is . . . image, image, image . . .*

There must be something else, she thought desperately as she poked at the clothes hanging on the rail, all the while aware of Jared waiting for her outside. Then a flash of red caught her eye — the velvet suit she'd bought for Becky's wedding. It wasn't something Jess would normally have bought, but Becky was successful and flamboyant, so she'd splashed out to fit in. In truth, she never expected to wear the suit again, much less in a work context. It was just so over the top, more like something

Lana would wear.

Lana. *Our top closer* Taffy said. That settled it. She'd bought shoes to match — where on earth were they? — and, having dressed in record time, she ran for the stairs.

Jared's eyes widened as she opened the car door. 'Nice look,' he said, in a tone that made her feel like the most powerful woman on the planet. It wasn't a feeling she was used to and it was quite intoxicating.

★   ★   ★

The house was a neatly kept mock-Tudor semi in a quiet street that was the epitome of suburbia. The Robsons were a rather sweet couple who Jess judged to be around retirement age. From the mantle-shelf pictures of adult offspring and grand-children, she guessed they'd lived there a long time, had gathered a lot of good memories in their home and so had decided to stay and improve the place, rather than move into something smaller, as so many people did at their age.

The couple confirmed all Jess's assumptions as soon as they began talking, the four of them standing around the coffee table in the warm and cosily cluttered living room. In fact, half their life story came out before Mr Robson made a joke about forgetting his manners and invited them to sit. His wife, June bustled off to the kitchen to make tea, and Mr Robson, who had introduced himself as Charles, popped out to join her for a moment.

Sinking into a bulky armchair, Jared gave Jess a smile and she smiled back, although she guessed they were thinking wildly different things. She read Jared's smile as, *Watch this — it will be a push over.*

She, on the other hand, was revelling in the unfamiliar sensation of sitting across the fire from Jared in a room so casually redolent of domestic bliss. He looked so handsome in his three-piece pinstripe suit, yet strangely content and at home, too.

Jess also felt good. If she'd had time to stop and think about the red suit, she'd have rejected it as too showy and gone with the cheap but safe charcoal number. But it felt good for once to be wearing something smart. The cut made her sit and stand more straight, made her aware of herself, not in the self-conscious way she expected but in a good way.

In her habitual jeans and trainers, she realised, she tended to take herself for granted, and perhaps Jared did, too. Jess Watkins, the girl who looked like she made the tea in a hairdressers. Well, she was glad Carl had pointed that out to her, for she felt certain Jared was looking at her differently now.

If only this house was theirs, she sighed inwardly just as the dream was broken when the Robsons came back with the tea.

Jess was surprised how gentle Jared

was with them. After all his motivational speaking and bell ringing in the office, she was curious to see how he operated.

There was no switching off of televisions — the Robsons were too polite to have left it on — and no kicking of window samples to show how tough the glass was. He was smooth, of course, but he was also far more understated and self-contained than she expected. Rather than pushing himself forward, he seemed to sit back and draw them towards him. She found it almost hypnotic to watch.

When he paid them a compliment, it sounded sincere, rather than sales talk and they were visibly flattered.

'The thing with compliments,' he explained to her later, 'is to never be general, always go for a specific detail. It's never, 'Oh, what great antiques you've got', it's 'Wow, this piece is really interesting. It really suits this room'. Gets them every time.'

That glib explanation to something

that looked so sincere made her remember her reaction to his compliment yesterday. *That's a lovely top, Jess. The colour really suits you.* Gets them every time, eh? Was it just sales talk — one of the thousand and one tricks he had for putting people at their ease? She was just beginning to wonder, when he confused her by adding, 'The trick is to say something you really mean.'

In the Robsons' front room, Jess had said little, giving Jared room to work his magic. She had a role to play, though, when he asked her to help him measure the windows.

The Robsons were a trusting pair, and they stayed in the living room, poring over the brochures Jared had given them while he and Jess wandered from room to room. As she held one end of the tape and he read off the measurements, it felt good to be working with him as a team. But as the Robsons' voices grew fainter, the impression of being alone in the house with him grew ever more dreamlike. Following Jared up the stairs to the darkened landing felt particularly unreal. As he led her into the bedroom and turned on the light, her heart was pounding so much she wondered if he could hear it. She hoped he didn't notice her eyes lingering on the bed.

What would it really be like to live with him, to wander into a bedroom each night and see his easy smile? To hear him swish the curtains on the rail, exactly as he was doing now, to get to the window.

The dreamlike feeling was all the stronger because Jared said not a word, apart from reading the measurements aloud to himself. She'd expected him to say something about how the sale was going, at least. She wished he would show some sign that he, too, was enjoying being with her in this unfamiliar and yet so cosy environment.

She almost prompted him. She thought of saying something, but his silence kept her silent. Forcing herself to stop playing happy families in her mind, she realised he was concentrating, preparing himself, focusing everything he had, not on the measuring, but on the part of the evening that was still to come: The Close.

Back in the living room, over more tea and biscuits, he gently went through the choices he'd asked them to consider while they pored over the brochures. 'So, shall we go for the white handles or the brass?'

Charles looked at June, 'It was the brass handles, wasn't it, love?'

Jess recognised the technique from Jared's pep talks in the office. *Always make it an either-or — do you prefer the Victorian or the Georgian? Shall I come Monday or Tuesday? It's called the win-win question.*

When Jess overheard that sort of thing in the office, she thought it sounded grindingly mechanical and unnatural, not to mention cynical. The art, she saw now, was the way Jared made a script sound spontaneous.

They don't buy the window, they buy the salesman — that was another one of his mantras — and with a tingling excitement in her stomach, Jess could see it happening in front of her. The Robsons were buying Jared like there was no tomorrow.

The 'close', when it came, was softer than Jess expected. He leaned across the coffee table and handed them the contract. He offered it, she noticed, to a space sort of midway between the couple where they sat side by side on the sofa, so they both took it together, each holding one edge of the paper, forcing them to lean closer together and read it as one.

While they were doing so, Jared sat back, wearing a smile as benign as a vicar at a christening, and said absolutely nothing. As the couple's eyes moved from the contract to each other, then back to the contract, Jess could hear the ticking of the carriage clock nestled amid the photos on the mantle-shelf. She realised she was holding her breath.

Eventually, Jared said, with that vicar's gentleness, 'I know I said the offer ends tonight, but I hate all that high-pressure nonsense. How about I leave that with you and pop by tomorrow evening to see what you think?'

Without waiting for an answer, he stood up and gave Jess the smallest of nods to indicate she do likewise.

As she rose, she saw Charles meet his wife's eyes, and saw something pass between them in a way that it only could between people who had known each other so intimately for so long. She found herself envying the couple's effortless compatibility.

So momentarily lost was she in her thoughts that it was like being jolted from a dream when Charles suddenly put the contract on the coffee table and stood up also. 'No, Mr King, there's no need to come back. I'll give you a deposit now.'

As they left the Robsons' front garden, Jess grabbed Jared's arm and hugged it in both of hers — she just couldn't stop herself. 'That was brilliant! You were brilliant! That was just so smooth!'

He gave her a mock-cool smile and said, mildly, 'I try.' Then he grinned, shook his arm loose from her embrace, and pulled out his car key.

As she tumbled into the passenger seat, Jess was still on a high. 'We can do it. You can do it. You can save the office.'

'It will need a lot more sales than that,' he reminded her.

'But you're just so good at this,' she enthused.

'They're not all as easy as that,' he smiled, as he started the engine.

'I just can't believe how gentle you were with them,' said Jess. 'I thought it was all hard sell.'

'They're all different,' said Jared. 'It's a matter of reading people. Knowing what's going to work with whom. With people like them, you don't push them, you let them come to you.'

'But that bit at the end, when you just stood up, did you know he was going to sign?'

Jared gave a small shrug as he drove. 'Pretty much. But if I had come back tomorrow, they'd have signed then.'

Jess lapsed into silence while she assimilated everything that had happened that evening. As the car purred through the dark streets, she was surprised by how cool Jared was being about the whole thing. What had happened to all that bell-ringing, pep-talk? She expected at least some of that, whereas it was her that had come out of there jumping in the air. She supposed everyone reacted to emotional moments in different ways.

At length, she said warmly, 'They were a nice couple, weren't they?'

Jared nodded, his eyes on the road.

Hardly believing she had the nerve to press the point, and definitely unable to look at him as she did so, she heard herself say, dreamily, 'Still so in love, even after all those years.'

Although she wasn't brave enough to take her eyes off the side window, she was positive she felt his gaze flick in her direction. Was it just a questioning glance, wondering what she was on about, or was he checking to see if she was dropping him a hint, giving him a come-on? Her neck and the side of her face burned under the scrutiny of his eyes, and she wondered if he could see it.

Eventually, he said, 'It makes you wonder, doesn't it?'

He drove in silence until he turned into her road and pulled up at the kerb. He killed the engine — a tiny act that made Jess's heart begin to pound

'Thanks for coming with me tonight,' he said.

'I enjoyed it.'

He hesitated. 'It's been a long time since I went out and closed a deal. I'm not sure I could have done it if you hadn't been there.'

Again she felt that sensation of connection, of two parts fitting together perfectly to make a whole.

She turned to look at him and, as she did so, every detail of the scene was suddenly so alive with possibility that she caught her breath. The two of them, the successful evening, the intimacy of the car, late at night, outside her door. She remembered hugging his arm outside the Robsons' house, spontaneous, not calculated, but it must have shown him she was interested. Then there was all the unsaid stuff as they walked around the house together, like walking through a sales brochure for a future they could have. Had he seen that — was he tempted?

She'd dropped another hint as they drove, talking about the Robsons' enduring love, letting him know that's what she dreamed of. Although she hadn't planned it, it was like she'd been laying out a sales pitch for him and, as her heart pounded, she knew with a sudden deep certainty that this was the moment — The Close — when he was either going to go for it or he wasn't.

Suddenly, it was like the Robsons' front room, neither of them speaking, neither of them breathing, while they waited for Mr Robson to make his decision. At that point Jess would have jumped in, just to break the silence and she would have blown it. But Jared just sat there, with that relaxed smile on his face, saying nothing, waiting for it to happen, letting it happen.

Was that all she had to do now? Just hold his eyes with hers, smile that smile at him, say nothing, and let it happen? She could barely stand the tension. She saw him take a breath, preparing to speak. Was it her imagination, or did she see him hesitate? Her senses were so hyper-alert that her brain was on overload. If it was anyone else, she might have jumped in, prompted him in some way. But this was too important. It had to come from him.

'Well,' he said, 'I'll see you tomorrow then, Jess.'

She didn't move, but the moment was slipping away. Was it too late to bring it back? She thought of asking him if he would like a coffee, but she knew it would sound desperate — and suppose he said no, or got embarrassed and made his excuses? She'd make a fool of herself.

Slowly, as she sat there, not moving, a cold realisation began to form in her stomach and she knew that she was eventually going to have to face it, so she might as well face it now.

It wasn't like she didn't know his circumstances. She knew what he was going through and understood that he wouldn't want to rush into a new relationship. But surely, if there was something to wait for, there would be some small sign in the meantime, some glimmer of interest? And, if she forced herself to put all her fantasies aside and look at the reality, she realised she just couldn't see one.

Take that moment when she grabbed his arm. Surely that was a moment when, in the giddiness of a successful sale, he could have given her a hug in return, or even a peck on the cheek? No one would think that inappropriate, even if just between friends, so there was no risk to their existing relationship and every chance for him to find out if she wanted to take things further. It was a win-win opportunity, to use one of his own phrases.

But, presented with an open door, he'd just shaken his arm free. Not in an unkind way but in the kindly way an indulgent but weary father might free himself from the hug of an over-excited kid. Was that how he saw her? She knew he liked her as a secretary, as a friend even, but she'd have to accept he simply didn't see her as anything more than that.

'Yeah,' she whispered. 'See you tomorrow.'

Grateful that she hadn't said anything to him, hadn't made any kind of move, and hadn't suffered the ultimate humiliation, she got out of the car and walked to her door. She didn't look back, because she didn't want him to see the stupid blur of mist across her eyes.

He waited at the kerb until she was safely indoors, then waited a bit longer until her light came on upstairs, before slowly driving away.

7

The next day, Jess was late, even by her standards. She knew Jared couldn't complain. She'd put in about four hours' unpaid overtime the previous evening, but that wasn't the real reason she was late, of course. If Jared was sensitive enough to know what the real reason was, he certainly didn't show it. He didn't even notice that the tea she took him was made without her usual loving care. She didn't take him a biscuit, either.

A voice in the back of her head said she was acting like they'd had a lovers' tiff when they'd never even been lovers. Her inner voice sarcastically asked her how she'd explain her behaviour if challenged. Her currently dominant wounded pride, however, had the satisfaction of pointing out that he hadn't even noticed there was anything wrong with her, let alone asked.

After sipping his tea with his usual 'Mmm', Jared said, 'I was thinking, after last night, that you ought to consider a career in sales, Jess.'

'Really,' she said flatly, without taking her eyes off her work.

'I just think you've got the poise for it. Wouldn't you say I'm right, Taffy?'

'You always know best, boss,' said the Welshman.

'Carl thinks it's all about being flash and persuasive; Lana thinks you have to dominate. But when it comes to people like the Robsons, it's really about making them like you, and you do that without trying. Look at that call you took, yesterday. Even when they're angry, people can't help liking you.'

But supposing you want to be more than liked, she thought, sulkily, just not in the mood for this conversation, she said with as much frosty politeness as she could, 'I'm quite happy as a secretary, thanks very much.'

'Just a thought,' said Jared. 'Are we

out of biscuits again, then?'

Jess gritted her teeth, stood up, walked to the kitchenette and picked up an unopened packet of digestives. She walked to his desk and whacked them onto the desktop just gently enough that the whole packet didn't turn to dust. Then she went back to her work.

Out of the corner of her eye, she saw Jared and Taffy exchange the sort of look that only ever passes between two men when a woman starts acting cranky for a reason they can't begin to understand.

* * *

It was later that afternoon that Carl told Jared he was leaving. Jess knew what he was about to do as soon as she noticed him hovering in front of Jared's desk. She picked up his apprehension and felt herself tensing as he cleared his throat and said, 'Could I have a word, boss? In private.'

Jared was busy with paperwork from

his solicitor. 'Can it wait, Carl?'

'Not really, boss. Perhaps we could just pop outside for a minute?'

Jared sighed, and followed the younger man downstairs.

At her desk, Jess wondered anxiously how it would go. She'd got over her strop, although she was still a little cold with him. She felt guilty about it, because she knew it wasn't his fault; he couldn't help the way he felt — or didn't feel — about her. He was still the same nice guy he'd always been.

But she couldn't help the way she felt, either. There was a dull ache of loss in her heart. It wasn't the loss of anything they'd actually had, because there never had been anything. It was the loss of possibility, the loss of hope, the loss of a maybe, and without that, the spark had gone. Now, when he smiled at her, or complimented her, instead of a quickening of her heart, she felt only the nasty stab of pain.

Alone in the office, she rubbed her eyes. She hadn't slept much last night as her mind kept going over things. She'd thought of handing in her notice, maybe taking up Carl's offer of the receptionist job. After all, she might be out of a job by the end of the month anyway. Why put herself though a painful experience until then?

By morning, she had decided not to be hasty. She still had a great working relationship with Jared. He made her feel part of a team in a way no other boss had. They had moments when they were more like friends — no, they *were* friends. Perhaps, in a few days, she'd be able to get herself back to a place where she could appreciate that for the wonderful thing it was. She should never have expected more in the first place.

She turned back to her desk and pretended to be getting on with her work when she heard two sets of footsteps and loud, hearty voices, coming back up the stairs.

'Congratulations are in order, Jess,' said Jared. 'Carl's got himself a new job.

Sales manager at Golden Windows.'

'Wow,' said Jess. She tried to look surprised, which actually wasn't too hard. Although, when she thought about it, she realised that Jared's cheerful reaction to the news wasn't as surprising as it would be in any other man. If he was angry about Carl's resignation, or gutted about it tipping the balance away from his efforts to save the office, he wasn't a man who would show it, not to Carl at any rate.

Then again, it was just as likely he was genuinely happy for Carl. Sometimes she thought he treated Carl like a son, and every father wants to see his son move on to greater things, doesn't he? Or maybe he felt, in his heart, that the office was doomed and Carl's new job meant one less redundancy to feel responsible for.

Wistfully, Jess wondered if she'd ever know what Jared was thinking.

'When do you start?' she asked Carl brightly, feigning interest.

'Tomorrow morning. You don't work

122

out your notice in this business.'

'He'd nick all our leads, wouldn't he?' Jared explained, good naturedly.

'If you had any leads!' Carl rejoined. 'So, come on, it's five o'clock. How about you two coming down the pub with me to celebrate?'

Jared was already behind his desk. 'I've got a lead to close later and all this to sort out. You two go and enjoy yourselves.'

'Jess?' Carl asked her, expectantly.

Caught off guard, Jess threw Jared a questioning look. His face was unreadable, but his words had felt like a shove.

'Why not?' she heard herself say. There was nothing for her here and it was only a drink, anyway.

'There's just one thing, boss,' said Carl. 'The Porsche isn't coming until Monday. Could I keep the Beamer till the end of the week?'

Jared snorted, but waved his hand in a way that said, *whatever*. Jess gave him a final glance, but his eyes were already in his legal papers. Whether they flicked up again, momentarily, just as she went through the door, she couldn't be certain.

She expected they'd walk to the pub, but when they reached the yard, Carl unlocked his car. He wanted to get the final use out of it, she supposed.

'To tell the truth, Jess, I'm starving. I know this nice little Italian restaurant. Do you fancy a bite? My treat.'

Jess hesitated, but only for a heartbeat. 'Why not?' she said again, and this time more like she meant it. She needed something to take her mind off Jared and, who knows, it might be fun. She didn't kid herself that there would ever be anything between herself and Carl, but he was a lot nearer her age than Jared was and, for all his faults, he did have a fun side.

The car was the twin of Jared's, and the off-white leather seat felt familiar. She could get used to this sort of luxury and she understood why Carl wanted to travel in style, even though it turned out that the distance was short enough that they could have walked it comfortably.

'It's got heated seats,' said Carl, as they pulled away. He pressed a button and she felt a welcome warmth spread through the small of her back.

The restaurant was small and vibrant. The waiter recognised Carl and sat them at a table in a booth. 'What would sir and madam like to drink?'

'Just orange juice for me,' said Jess.

'Me too,' said Carl. Seeing her surprise, he said, 'I'm not really a drinker. I had a few in the pub the other night, but that was to fit in with that laddish sales culture Jared and Taffy like. All that hard-sell, 'We're the best' bell-ringing stuff. There won't be any of that in my showroom. You don't need it.'

Their drinks arrived and Carl clinked his glass against hers and said, 'This is the first time we've really had the chance to sit down and have a chat, isn't it? Away from work, I mean. It's different when you can get away from the office and all the politics and the roles everyone plays. You come somewhere like this and you can be yourself.'

'So let's not talk about work, then,' Jess reminded him, with a smile.

'Hear, hear,' said Carl. 'So what do you do at the weekends?'

If the Carl across the table was the real Carl, he was a lot easier to be with than the one she knew from the office. Relaxed, attentive, courteous, considerate. He liked some of the music she liked, which was rare for a bloke, and he went to the same resort in Spain last year that she had. They recalled moments from films they'd both seen.

Of course, she knew what he was doing. She'd seen Jared do it to the Robsons and Carl had learned from Jared. He was charming her because that was what he did for a living. As the evening wore on, she took a playful delight in inwardly noticing some of the tricks. She could almost hear Jared's voice running a commentary with his favourite phrases.

But a wounded heart can stomach a lot of charming and Carl played the tricks so well it was easy to forget it was charm and start to believe it was real, especially if you wanted to believe it. After all, what was wrong with getting a little lift, if only for a while? Besides, that handsome face and blue eyes of his were no hardship to look at.

Eventually, they decided to risk a glass of white wine. 'Just the one, as I'm driving,' said Carl. 'But you can have another if you like.'

By the time the restaurant started playing Angels by Robbie Williams, Jess's wounded heart was feeling very soothed indeed, and just a little open once more to thoughts of romance. As the song reached its stirring emotional climax, she found herself drifting into a wistful little daydream in which the handsome man across the table was just a little older with dark hair instead of blond . . .

But who said you could have

everything? Perhaps Jared had deliberately pushed her towards Carl and perhaps she should thank him. Who knows how long she might have gone on fantasising about the unobtainable when a girl should have her eyes open for people who are actually interested. Every no leads to a yes, as Jared said. Funny how it was always his words that came into her mind, though.

Eventually, Carl called for the bill. 'Why don't we drive by the office?'

'To see Jared?' asked Jess.

'Not that office!' Carl laughed. 'The new office.'

When Carl slid the BMW up to the curb by the new showroom, Jess had to admit Golden Windows lived up to its name. It was a huge, glass-fronted building with all the lights on inside, gleaming off pristine displays, leather-topped desks and deep pile carpet. Silent and new, the showroom looked as if it were shrink-wrapped, waiting for Carl to break the seal.

'That would be your desk,' Carl

pointed. 'The one just inside the door. The first thing everybody sees.'

His voice sounded closer than it had. Jess turned her head to find him leaning across the car towards her. He may just have been trying to get a better view through the window on her side. Perhaps that really was all he originally intended. But, suddenly, their faces were very close. She could see the long lashes around those almost luminous blue eyes and the individual strands of his pale blond hair. The skin on his lean cheek was as soft as a boy's. His lips were surprisingly pink and delicate.

Their eyes met, he smiled, and her heart quickened as she saw what was going to happen next. Slowly, he leaned in. She could have turned her head, so that he kissed her cheek, but . . . she wasn't quite sure why she didn't. If she'd taken time to think about it, she might have said she was curious. Or, if she faced the truth, that Jared had left her feeling unloved. She wanted so much to be loved. She let Carl put those soft lips to hers, she closed her eyes — and she felt nothing.

Nothing except a hand trailing over her knee. Gently but firmly, she moved his hand and was relieved he got the message first time.

'It's been a lovely evening,' she said, slightly flustered. 'But . . . '

He moved back, with a nod that said there was no need to explain. In fact, he didn't look particularly perturbed. She could almost hear the familiar line, *Some you win* . . . He offered to drive her home, but she insisted she'd be okay from here. As she got out of the car, he said, 'What about the job?'

'I think I'll say no to that, too.'

He didn't argue and as she watched the sleek black car purr away, she wondered what she was saying no to. Carl was okay, in his way, and the new showroom was as slick as he was, but it was top show, all of it.

Glad of the cool air to clear her head, she stuck her hands in her pockets and walked along the high street. Some of the shops were lit up and empty, like Golden Windows. Most were in darkness.

After a while, she wondered why she was walking this way when she lived in the opposite direction. Then, up ahead and across the road, she saw the open sash window above the betting shop. Jared was leaning out, shirt cuffs loosely folded, forearms resting on the sill; a pose that suggested he'd been there some time, gazing out at nothing much in particular.

She stopped in the shadow of a doorway. He hadn't seen her, and wouldn't if she walked no further. Dramatically back-lit by the lights of the office, with the streetlamps picking out his features, he looked like the hero of a movie and that Robbie Williams song, stuck on 'play' in her head, provided the soundtrack. As Robbie twisted the emotions in her stomach, Jared looked so strong but so alone. Not happy, she thought, not happy by a long stretch, but stoical, just him and his pride, that impenetrable pride that protected him and kept him lonely.

What are you thinking about, Jared? she wondered. What do you want?

8

Jess was carrying supplies of milk and biscuits up the stairs when she heard the shouting. Quickening her step, she burst in to find Taffy verbally laying into Jared across his desk.

'You knew about this all along, didn't you?' The back of the Welshman's neck was as red as a bus. 'I've got a wife and kids to support! How dare you not tell us about this!'

As Jess dumped the supermarket bag on her desk, Jared glanced in her direction. He may just have been looking for help, but the thought that he suspected her as the source of leaked information stung her deeply.

'Don't look at her, boyo!' Taffy was leaning across Jared's desk, his finger pointed like a gun. 'I called by the factory. They all know we're being closed. Everybody knows except us poor mugs!' Jared tried to get a word in, but it was like trying to stop Niagara Falls with a bucket. 'We could have been looking for new jobs while you're playing us along like it's business as usual then come the end of the month you'd kick us in the teeth!'

If anyone looked about to kick someone in the teeth, it was Taffy. 'If you think I'm wasting my time around here for another two weeks you've got another think coming! You can stick your job right now!'

If he'd been on television, Taffy would have stormed out the door at that point. As it was he had to go to his desk and bang the drawers in and out, steaming and snorting like a bull as he threw his few personal possessions into his briefcase.

Jared watched him, unspeaking, holding everything in. He was good at rallying speeches, Jess noted, but he didn't do begging or chasing lost causes. She admired his dignity. At that moment, though, she couldn't help wondering if silence was the right move.

While Taffy fumed and banged about at his desk, Lana stalked across the office and threw a lead card on Jared's desk.

'You can count me out, too!' As she strutted haughtily to the door, she spat over her shoulder, 'That dispute was your fault, not mine!'

There were two other salesmen in the office. Jess heard one of them say, 'I'm going down to Golden Windows to see if Carl's got any jobs.'

As Taffy bundled his stuff under his arm and charged, cursing and flame-faced, out the door, Angie turned to Rudi. 'No point us getting leads if there are no salesmen to close them. Come on, the curtain's coming down.'

As Angie grabbed her coat, Rudi put on his best Broadway accent and said, 'So long, boss. It was nice knowin' ya.'

A few minutes later, as the final clatter of footsteps echoed down the stairs, Jared and Jess were alone in the office. The only sound was the noise of the high street, drifting in through the window, and the distant sound of cars being started and driven out of the yard downstairs. At length, Jared let out a long, slow breath. Then he turned to Jess, where she had sat down, in shock, at her desk.

'So what are you still doing here?' He glared at her.

'I work here,' said Jess. 'What about you?'

For a moment, he continued to glare at her. Then his face cracked into a smile. Hers did, too and soon the smiles became laughter as all the hidden tension came out.

For Jess, it was more than just the tension of the past few minutes. After the coolness that had existed between her and Jared since last week, she was relieved to find they were friends again. Realising how stupid she'd been to let her crazy romantic fantasies get in the way of the real bond between them, she wiped a tear of joy from the corner of her eye.

As his chuckles subsided, Jared said, 'You and me against the world?'

'You bet!' she replied in the elation of the moment. But it didn't change the fact that unless something pretty dramatic happened in the next couple of weeks they wouldn't have an office to work in. 'Can we still do it?'

They both looked at the big white sales board. Jared had been busy in the past week, and chalked up another two sales. But Carl's sale to the Hattersleys had fallen through and been crossed out. With Jared now the only remaining salesman, the board told a gloomy story. She was buoyed to find that Jared was a bad listener.

'We can but try, Jess.' Thoughtfully, he picked up the lead card that Lana had thrown on his desk and another one that was already there. He tapped the edges of the cards together.

'Well, we've got two appointments at the same time this evening. I may be a super-salesman, but even I can't be in two places at once. How do you fancy going out and closing a deal?'

'Me?' Jess squeaked in horror. 'I couldn't sell anything!'

'Of course you can!' Jared enthused. 'You've been out with me and seen how it's done and, like I said to you last week, the real skill lies in getting people to like you. You'll be halfway there before you start.'

'But I don't know anything about windows!'

'I'll teach you!'

'Between now and this evening?' she spluttered.

'Who said it would take that long? First of all, let's get you kitted out. Have you got a briefcase?'

Beginning to catch his enthusiasm, despite the craziness of the situation, she shook her head and watched as he began rummaging in a low desk drawer, eventually pulling out a dusty leather zip-around file. Crossing the office to Lana's desk, he said, 'Right, here are some brochures, price list, tape measure . . . can you drive?'

'Yes.' She'd learned in her brother's car and passed her test as soon as she left school, although why she'd bothered she wasn't sure. For a while she'd driven her brother's hand-me-down Fiesta until an MOT-tester told her it was only worth scrapping. By that time, she'd left home and hadn't been able to afford a car since.

'You can have Carl's. He dropped the keys back today.'

'The BMW?' she squeaked.

'Can't have you going on the bus.' Jared picked up a rag and began wiping the names of the other sales people from the shiny white sales board. He picked up a red marker and wrote her name under his own. 'After me, you have just been officially promoted to our top closer — and the job comes with a car.'

He handed her one of the lead cards. 'You better take Lana's. Kim Hunt. Sounds like a woman on her own. Posh road, though, so she'll probably be quite up market.'

He cast his eyes over Jess and said, 'Don't let her intimidate you. Wear your red suit. You look really hot in it.'

A couple of weeks ago, Jess's heart would have skipped when he said that. His words still tugged at her insides, but now it only caused a twinge of pain and left an ache of sadness. She knew he meant the compliment. But she also knew it meant nothing to him. It was like the way he'd compliment a client on a painting. It didn't mean he wanted to take it home with him.

'Jared . . . ?' she began, because it no longer seemed like there was so much at stake. 'Why did your last secretary leave?'

'Ena?' He looked puzzled, like it was a lifetime ago. Eventually, he said, 'Her hip went and she couldn't get up and down the stairs anymore. I shouldn't be unkind, but it was a small mercy, really, because her eyes were already going, as you could probably tell from the paperwork. She was about seventy-five.'

Jess shrieked with laughter.

'What's so funny?'

'Nothing!' Jess had a hand over her mouth, trying to suppress her mirth.

'Come on, out with it,' he pressed her. Then, when she shook her head, 'Wait a minute, let me guess . . . someone said something, didn't they? I bet it was Carl.'

'I'm not saying!' Jess giggled. She was enjoying having a secret and Jared determined to get it out of her. She didn't often get the chance to be playful with him. It felt close and flirtatious and she could see it in his eyes.

'Something about me and my secretary . . . ' He pondered, playing along and acting as if he were really determined to work out the secret.

Jess could keep him in suspense no longer. 'He said you were having an affair!' She said it with a grin, because they were playing and it felt safe to do so, and because, well, what could be more ridiculous than Jared having an affair with seventy-five-year-old Ena with her dodgy eyes and hip? But Jared suddenly wasn't playing anymore. His face darkened and he leaned back from her. He walked away and went around behind his desk, as if he felt safer there.

Jess felt the smile slipping off her face as she wondered what on earth she'd said wrong. Surely he and Ena weren't really having an affair?

At length, it was Jared's turn to put her out of her suspense. Looking away and rubbing the back of his neck, he said, 'It wasn't me who had the affair. It was Suzanne.'

The words couldn't have hit Jess harder if she'd been wronged herself. A bolt of hurt on his behalf went through her from head to toe.

The instant the initial shock had passed through her, she wanted to hug him and soothe his pain. She took a step forward, but, even as she did so, something selfish held her back. What if he rejected her, shied away from her embrace or just coldly disentangled himself from her arms? With a man like Jared, dare she take the risk?

'That's awful,' she breathed. She took another step forward, torn between love and fear. But already she saw that he was pulling himself back together. If there had been a moment of vulnerability when she could have hugged him and he might have welcomed it, it was slipping away.

He gave a little shrug. 'It happens.'

She watched him, unspeaking, wondering what on earth she could say. The expression on her face must have had a softening effect on him, however. Because, after needlessly straightening a couple of papers on his desktop, he met her eyes and said, 'It was a guy she works with. She's high up in an events management firm. Long hours, late nights. Business trips.' He sat down and looked away, as if picturing it all.

Jess sat across the desk from him, the closest she dared to get, although her heart and mind were right over there on his side of the desk with him. 'You tried to keep the marriage going?' she ventured in a whisper. 'For Josh's sake?'

He nodded slowly, then glanced at her, as if deciding whether to tell her more. She felt another little stab of rejection as he clearly decided not to. At length, he seemed to gather himself, shaking off his thoughts of the past.

'So how did you get on with Carl the other night?'

The change of mood caught Jess off guard. Having been lost in her own thoughts, she looked up quickly and was struck by a vaguely accusatory look in Jared's eyes. The look was in such contrast to his casual tone that she wondered if he were really changing the subject at all. He'd been betrayed by Suzanne, so was that why he'd pushed her towards Carl — to test her in some way?

'He offered me a job,' she said simply.

Jared nodded thoughtfully and she supposed the fact she was still here told him she'd turned Carl down, but with a wry smile, he said, 'I suppose you took one look at that fancy new showroom and decided you had better prospects here?'

Jess felt a flood of relief to be getting back to the playful tone they'd shared earlier. 'Well, I've just been promoted and given a company car, so things aren't going too badly.'

He chuckled and she was glad to see that momentary look in his eyes was gone. 'Seriously, though, Jess. The chances of keeping the office going aren't that great. Perhaps it would be a good idea to keep your eyes open for something else.'

'You're not giving up, are you?'

Jared rallied indignantly. 'Of course not.'

'Then neither am I.' He gave her an appreciative look, and the sensible part of her knew she should have left the subject there. But, as her mouth became suddenly dry, she realised there was something inside her that just wouldn't stay unsaid. 'I won't desert you, Jared.'

Her voice cracked as she said it, but she forced herself to meet his eyes the whole time. She saw her sincerity hit him like a small punch in the forehead. He looked a little taken aback but, as usual, he hid his feelings so well that the reaction would have been easy to miss.

'I know you won't.' He stood up briskly, popped out his cufflinks and began rolling his sleeves. 'Now, brace yourself Jess. I've got two hours to teach you everything I know.'

To her disappointment, he lifted a doubled-glazed window onto his desk and said, 'Now this is what we call the . . .'

* * *

The driver's seat was very different to the passenger seat, Jess found. Having previously driven a tiny hatchback, the interior of the BMW felt the size of a small flat and the exterior the size of an ocean liner. She didn't know how she'd get it out of the yard without scratching it, let alone park it somewhere. She could barely see over the steering wheel and Carl had left the seat so far back, she couldn't reach the pedals.

Forcing herself to recall everything she remembered about driving, she searched under the seat for a bar or lever that would let her slide it forward. There wasn't one. Well, there had to be a way of moving the seat. Eventually, she found an oval-shaped switch on the side. She twisted it and her knees rose with an electronic hum. She twisted it the other way and her hips were lifted. She pushed it and the seat slid forward like a magic carpet.

After much moving in every direction, she eventually found herself in a position where she not only had good visibility, but actually felt in command of the car.

Gingerly, she pressed the accelerator

and found that the big car was more forgiving of her rusty driving than her old banger had been.

By the time she'd nosed out of the yard and then swished more confidently along the high street, she began to think that perhaps she could actually do this. By the time she'd stopped off to change into her red suit, spent a little time on her make-up and added a spray of perfume for luck, she'd revised her opinion of why Carl and Jared put so much value on the right clothes and the right car. Growing comfortable with the accoutrements of a rich and successful person actually made her feel more competent.

The house was in a different league to the one she had visited with Jared. It was a flat-fronted Georgian property that screamed money. But in the BMW Jess felt strangely unintimidated. There was a wide drive at the front, and as she crunched onto the gravel and parked next to a similar dark saloon, she thought, *So this is what it feels like to be a successful woman coming home of an evening.*

Closing the car door with an expensive click, she tucked her zip-around file under her arm and felt her high heels forcing her into a more upright, confident posture. Taking her time to get a feel for the place, she stepped up to the front door and prepared to meet the wealthy woman who lived here as Jared would — in the frame of mind of an equal.

The door was opened by a relaxed, good looking man in his thirties.

'Mr Hunt?' she said, slightly surprised. 'I'm Jessica Watkins from Brachan Windows.'

'Hi,' he smiled. 'Come in.' He didn't have an overly posh accent, she noted, just that completely relaxed assurance you saw in celebrities or royals who were so wealthy and good looking they'd never had to worry about much in their entire lives.

'I was expecting someone called Lana,' he said in a not especially concerned, Hugh Grant-ish sort of way as he led her into a wide hall.

And I was expecting a woman, thought Jess. As much as she fought not to show it, she realised that, now she was in here with the door closed firmly behind her, she was as intimidated as she could be by this man's house, his wealth, his handsome features. She was certain that as soon as she spoke he'd discover she was a fake saleswoman, with a borrowed car, who didn't know the first thing about windows.

She noticed there were framed gold discs on the wall beside the stairs and wondered if he were famous, although she'd never seen his face in the celebrity mags. He led her into a generously proportioned lounge and turned on the lights to reveal a white baby grand piano in one corner.

She sensed from the stillness of the house that they were alone.

'Is Mrs Hunt home?' she asked. He looked bemused. 'Kim Hunt?' Jess prompted and he smiled at what was obviously a common mistake.

'I'm Kim,' He explained. 'Sadly, there is no Mrs Hunt, more's the pity.'

'I'm surprised!' Jess blurted nervously and, feeling flustered for sounding so stupid, immediately made things worse by saying, 'I mean, a good looking guy like you . . . ' *Shut up!* she told herself, ' . . . in a house like this . . . ' *Shut up right now!* ' . . . I'd have thought you'd be beating them off!'

By the time she'd finished digging that hole for herself, her face was so red that they both burst out laughing, which was a relief, she supposed, although it scarcely made the moment any less cringe-worthy.

'Well, I suppose I am,' he said, and somehow had the ability to make it sound self-deprecating, which was a neat trick, Jess had to admit.

'I suppose what I'm trying to say,' he went on, 'is that I just never seem to meet the kind of women I don't want to beat off. The trouble with the business I'm in is that, when people find out who you are, the first thing they're interested in is what you can do for them. Then, when they see you've got a nice house and a bit of money, well, I'm sure you get the picture. What I've always wanted is someone who just wants me for me.'

He looked at her with eyes so soulful that Jess felt herself sway. Forcing herself to get a grip, she said, 'What business are you in then?'

'I write scores and theme tunes for TV shows.'

'Anything I'd know?'

Almost shyly, Kim stood by the piano and, with one hand, picked out a simple seven note refrain that Jess had heard every week for as long as she could remember.

'That was you?' She exclaimed.

'How about this one?' said Kim, and picked out the intro to a well known detective show.

'Oh my God!' Jess had never met anyone famous before and heard herself squealing like a schoolgirl.

'Everyone knows the tune, nobody knows my name,' Kim smiled, wistfully. 'But you didn't come here to hear the story of my life. Let me show you the windows I need a quote for.'

Glad to let him take charge of the appointment, Jess followed Kim to the large sash windows.

'The trouble with these old places is they look nice but they're so drafty. So I want everything at the front changed to double glazing. Hardwood frames in a sympathetic period style, of course. Then . . . if you'll follow me through here . . . ' he led her through a spacious kitchen, turning on the light as he went. 'I want a nice conservatory off the back. I'm thinking Victorian, but I expect you'll show me some brochures?'

'Of course.'

Suddenly, he shot her a look that said he was a lot sharper than his laid-back, almost whimsical manner suggested. 'What kind of wood do you use? Oak or cedar wood?'

Jess didn't even know they did wood

windows, her brochures were all for plastic. But, before she could panic, she remembered what Jared had told her to say if she found herself on the spot. With almost the assurance of Jared himself, she looked Kim in the eye and said, sweetly, 'Which would you prefer?'

From there, Jess managed to bluff it with ease. Falling back on a plan Jared had talked her through, she explained that because this would be a specialist order she'd have to make notes, go away and come back with a price later. To her relief, Kim turned out to be knowledgeable enough to give her very clear instructions on what he wanted and even helped her with the tape measure while she measured up.

Afterwards, he made her tea and, as they chatted comfortably in the kitchen, she realised how much she was enjoying the evening. She'd expected his wealth and success to be a barrier between them — that he'd look down on her in some way — but he treated her just like any normal person. Jess heard herself using some of Jared's conversational tricks to get Kim talking about himself and quickly found that they were getting on well. It was more like a social visit than work and by the time she'd finished a second cup of tea she was surprised to see how late it was; she'd been there three hours.

'Well, I'll come back with some prices for you,' she said at last. 'How about tomorrow evening?'

'I'm afraid I'm recording tomorrow. How about Friday?'

'Friday it is, then.'

'Come about seven, and I'll cook you dinner.'

The invitation caught Jess off guard. Then she remembered Jared's first rule of selling — the most important thing is that they like you.

Well, considering that Kim supposedly spent his days beating off unwanted females — and it really didn't seem that far fetched — she guessed she must be ticking some of the right boxes.

'Okay,' she said, trying to casually

make it sound as if rich and talented men asked her to dinner every day.

As Kim stood in his front doorway and Jess felt his gaze on her back as she walked away across the darkened gravel, she was so glad she had a thirty thousand pound car to get into. As she drove away, she was euphoric, convinced she'd be able to pull the deal off.

As she cruised through the dark, deserted streets, however, she found herself reflecting more deeply upon the evening. At the time, she had barely noticed it happening, but looking back, she realised that the experience of the past three hours had shown her a different version of herself.

Having begun the evening as a girl playing the part of a successful woman, she had, at least for a while, actually become that woman. She felt confident, assured and wealthy on the inside — and it was a feeling she liked.

As she smoothly handled the controls of the BMW, like it was the kind of car she belonged in, she pictured herself at the kind of parties a man like Kim might throw, chatting with assurance to the sort of rich, successful people he would know, before going home to a similarly elegant house of her own. This Jess would be at home in that world.

As she turned into her road, however, she began to have that feeling you get when you wake from a really good dream. Almost everything about the evening was an illusion. She wasn't really a friend of Kim's — she was only in his house because she was doing her job. It wasn't even her real job since she had fallen into it through a twist of fate and faked her way through with a borrowed car and some patter learned parrot fashion from Jared.

But did that mean the new woman Jess had found inside herself was an illusion, too? Suppose the dinner with Kim went well. Suppose — and this was purely for the sake of argument — suppose they got together and she ended up living in his house and driving a car like this for real? Would she become this version of Jess forever, or would she still be faking it?

As she parked, she thought of the Jess she was around Becky and the Jess she was around Jared. The girl on the sidelines, the eager helpmate, helping someone else shine, the jeans and trainers Jess who looked like a girl who made the teas in a hairdressers, the girl who was happiest living in a dream world because the thought of trying to turn her dreams into reality was just too bloomin' scary.

That Jess and this Jess were like two different women, each with a different view of life — each, she began to wonder, with a different destiny?

As she left the BMW at the kerb, conscious that she was leaving part of this evening's Jess behind, and crossed the pavement to her door, her thoughts turned as usual to Jared. There was a man who had lost his house, his marriage and in all probability was about to lose his job. He was reduced to sleeping in his office. But, even without

all those trappings he was still unshake-
ably Jared. In fact, Jess couldn't
imagine any circumstances, rich or
poor, in which he'd be anyone other
than his calm, kind, competent and
completely rock solid self.

The question she asked herself as she
let herself into her tiny rented room
was, who was the real Jess Watkins? As
she took off her red suit — the last part
of that Jess — turned off the light and
crawled into bed, she hugged her pillow
and wished she knew.

9

Jess was late for work despite the BMW. In fact, road-works in the high street made her later than if she'd walked. As she squeezed the brake and halted behind the backed-up traffic, she glanced to her left and realised she was outside the Golden Windows show-room.

Behind the wide glass frontage, everything looked bright and bustling; a pristine, forward-looking opposite to the shabby, closure-threatened Brachan Windows office. A young and clearly very much in love couple were browsing the sample windows — newly-weds, Jess guessed, choosing improvements for their first home. She felt a stab of envy of their contentment, as they held hands while he opened and closed one of the windows. No doubt they'd soon be starting a family.

Just inside the doors was the desk Carl had offered to Jess. Behind it, he'd installed the drop-dead gorgeous receptionist he wanted and had kitted her out in the Prada he'd offered Jess. The girl wore it well, Jess had to admit. She was model thin, with a coquettish face so perfectly made-up it might have been airbrushed for the cover of a magazine. Her yellow blonde hair was so expensively tended it almost sparkled.

The girl was simpering flirtatiously as Carl leaned over her shoulder with one hand on the back of her chair, their faces were close as he put his hand over hers and steered her mouse to show her something on her computer.

The blonde didn't have his full attention, however, because he suddenly glanced towards the street and did a little double take as he recognised his former company car. He leaned forward a little more, so he could see who was driving.

Their eyes met and, after his initial blink of surprise, Jess guessed they were both thinking the same thing — how it could so easily have been Jess sitting where the blonde girl was now. Jess wondered if he'd taken Blondie to that Italian restaurant yet, or leaned in for that first kiss? The girl didn't look like she'd push him away. Perhaps they'd soon be an item, like the couple checking out the windows on the other side of the showroom. They certainly looked good together.

And where would Jess be in a couple of weeks? Probably looking for a new job, with a boss who wouldn't be anywhere near as nice as Jared.

She didn't doubt Jared would find a new job easily enough, and she wondered if they'd ever see each other once they no longer shared an office. Maybe once, for a drink, she guessed. Her heart would give a little jump when she walked in and saw him, looking as smart and handsome as ever, and then, as always, she'd remember they were just friends. She'd ask him how things were going, and he'd say 'Fine'. He'd ask how she was getting on and she'd say 'Good'. She'd ask about his divorce and he'd say it was going through as well as you could expect. Eventually, they'd say, 'We must do this again sometime', but it would feel forced and awkward. After all, how many friendships did she keep up with people from previous jobs? You just didn't, did you?

An angry honk jolted Jess from her reverie. Realising the traffic had moved forward, she slipped the shiny, walnut-covered gear-stick into first and drove on.

* * *

When Jess trotted up the stairs to the office, her heart soared to see how much energy Jared was putting into saving the office. He'd scrawled another sale in red marker on the whiteboard. He'd also promoted the three most promising door-knockers to closers. As Jess came in, they were sitting in a semi-circle while Jared balanced a window on his desk and gave them the crash-course he'd given her.

The new recruits were going to have to keep knocking on doors to generate their own leads and then convert them to sales as well, but Jared told them they could do it and promised them riches if they did.

'Meet Jess, our newest closer,' he said, as she walked to her desk. 'Two weeks ago Jess was walking to work and had never sold anything in her life. Today she's driving a top range BMW.'

On cue, Jess held up her car key, dangling from its leather fob, and posed hand on hip, like a game show hostess. She couldn't help feeling the effect would have been stronger if she'd been wearing her red suit instead of her jeans and trainers. But the distinctively shaped Beamer key couldn't be argued with and the three spotty teenagers in cheap suits looked suitably impressed.

'So who's the best?' Jared shouted, as he reached for his bell.

'We are!' Jess chanted back until all

the new salesmen were joining in just as enthusiastically.

As the trio headed for the stairs with their heads full of half-remembered facts about windows and big dreams of flash cars, Jess was pleased with her performance. It was completely spontaneous but in moments like that she and Jared were so in tune it was like they had rehearsed. What a shame, she thought wistfully, that he was content to leave such teamwork at the office door. The thought of being able to read each other's thoughts like that in every area of life made the wasted opportunity seem criminal.

Shaking off the thought, she said brightly, 'You got last night's sale?'

'Only a pair of French doors. But we're getting there. What about you?'

Jess pulled up a chair in front of his desk and filled him in. As he looked at the notes she passed him, he said, 'This is specialist stuff. We'd have to use a different factory, but I know a place that could do it. PG won't mind as long as there's a profit margin. It won't come cheap, though. How much money do you think this guy's got?'

'A lot,' said Jess.

Jared reached for a calculator. 'In that case, let's start pricing it up.' When he'd finished, he said, 'This will be a big commission for you.'

She hadn't even thought about commission. When he told her she stood to collect as much from one deal as she earned in a month as secretary, she began to understand why the salesmen got so excited about closing a deal and why they didn't mind facing rejection after rejection in between. At the same time, she realised the deal wasn't closed yet. Kim hadn't even seen the price, let alone decided to buy.

She guessed Jared saw her sudden uncertainty for he said, 'Would you like me to close it for you? Still giving you the commission, of course.'

Jess was tempted but said, 'No. I want to see it through.'

Jared smiled like he recognised a new

salesperson getting the bug. What he couldn't see was the real reason closing the deal was so important to her, and that was to find out if she really could be the Jess she'd been last night.

'When are you going back?' he asked.

'Friday. He invited me to dinner.'

Jared's eyebrows shot up. Was that just a smidgeon of jealousy in his eyes? He certainly sounded protective as he said, 'Are you sure this guy's above board? If I'd known he was a bloke on his own, I'd never have sent you. I just assumed Kim was a woman.'

'Me too, but he seems harmless.'

'I could come with you,' Jared offered. 'I wouldn't say a word. Let you handle the whole thing.'

'Thanks but I'm a big girl. I'll be fine,' she teased.

'As long as you're home by ten!' he played along, mock stern. Then, with a warmth that surprised her, added, 'I wish I'd met you ten years ago, Jess.'

'Is that because you've got a thing about school uniforms?' she shot back saucily, but the joke came out of nervous excitement. He'd never said anything about the two of them before and her heart was racing at the thought of what might be coming next.

Flustered, Jared said, 'What I meant was, I wish I was twenty four or twenty five and you were the age you are now.'

Ten years ago . . . before he married Suzanne . . . ? Jess's heartbeat was drumming in her ears.

'I should have done what PG Brachan did. Start my own window company. If I'd had someone with your enthusiasm to back me up, I really think we could have done it. But it's so hard finding people to trust, and I didn't have the nerve to go it alone. Then, when Josh came along . . . ' He gazed away into his missed opportunities.

Jess's romantic aspirations were so crushed to find that, once again, he was thinking of her only in a work context, that it took her a moment to latch onto the positive part of what he said.

'Couldn't you still do that?' She asked, quickly. 'Start your own business, I mean, if PG closes the office?'

As usual, though, Jared's moment of soul-baring was fleeting and as she spoke, she could see that, once again, she had missed her opening. Jared sucked his teeth and said, 'Some things you either do at the time, or you don't do them at all. Anyway, now that I've been out closing deals again, I don't feel so bad about getting another job. For a moment, I did wonder if I still had it. Speaking of which — ' Jared looked at his watch. 'If you'll excuse me, I've just got time to move this stuff before my next appointment.'

Standing quickly, he picked up his rolled sleeping bag and, hefting it awkwardly by a strap that held it together, grabbed a sports bag with his free hand.

'Let me help you,' said Jess, following him around his desk.

'No, I can manage,' Jared insisted. But with his hands full he couldn't stop her grabbing a bin liner full of his clothes and following him down the narrow, wooden stairs.

'Are you moving back home?' she blurted.

A hearty laugh told her how ridiculous that thought was. In the yard he opened the boot of his car and threw the sleeping bag inside. 'I've found a room to rent around the corner. It's hardly the Ritz but it's better than the office floor.'

He headed back upstairs to get more of his stuff and she charged up after him like a shadow. When they'd crammed the last of his belongings onto the backseat, Jared thanked her and opened the driver's door.

'Shall I come and help you unpack?' Jess cursed the neediness in her voice. Surely she could sound slightly less unloved and abandoned?

He gave her a smile that looked like sympathy. 'No, you stay and hold the fort. I'll go on to my appointment and call back into the office later.'

As she watched the sleek car pull out of the yard, Jess caught sight of herself practically wringing her hands, like a sailor's sweetheart left standing on the shore. Never mind not inviting her round, he hadn't even told her his new address. Suddenly she hated herself for what she let herself become around Jared and knew she couldn't go on like this. She remembered how she felt with Kim last night. It was time to decide who the real Jess was.

★ ★ ★

The next day, Jared came into the office looking especially pleased. 'I've just bumped into Taffy. Carl's given him a job.'

Jess loved the way he cared about his people.

'Would you mind if I take some time off tomorrow?' she asked. 'I want to get my hair cut before my appointment.'

She choose a style similar to Carl's receptionist; a short but sophisticated look that went with the BMW. She didn't want Kim to think she owned only one suit, so she teamed her new hairdo with her little black Friday night dress. Like the red suit, it was something she'd never normally have considered as work-wear, but in the strange new world where this Jess worked, she'd found that different rules applied. After all, it was Friday night, and as well as going to work, she was going to dinner.

She checked her new look in the mirror and found that, to use Jared's words, she did indeed look 'hot'.

And Kim certainly seemed to think so, too. As he took her coat, she noticed him deeply inhale her perfume. 'If you'll pardon my saying so,' he said in that Hugh Grant-ish way of his, 'that new hairstyle really suits you.'

The smells wafting from the kitchen were delicious and he'd put on some romantic music, softly, in the background. It was a pretty corny thing to do, Jess thought with a smile, but it was still nice when a guy made an effort.

'Food will be a while,' he said. 'So have you got all the information you were going to bring me?'

They went into the living room and sat facing each other across a stylish coffee table where Jess put on a sales presentation she and Jared had spent most of the week rehearsing to the last detail. Jared had been to the factory and obtained specialist brochures and photographs of previous work. He'd got her a sample hardwood window corner, so she could show Kim exactly how it was put together and even how the wood was prepared and treated. She and Jared had then spent ages role-playing the questions Kim was likely to ask and how she should answer them.

Although neither Jess nor Jared had come right out and admitted it to each other, she guessed they both knew that, despite Jared's almost superhuman efforts, with only a week to go, they had little chance of saving the office from closure, but he'd told her that even if it did close, Kim's order would still go through head office and Jess would get her commission. She assumed that since she was likely to be out of a job, Jared figured the least he could do was try to ensure she came away with a lump sum. She, of course, hadn't told him what this deal really meant to her.

At last, after she had answered all Kim's questions with aplomb, he asked, 'So how much is all this going to cost me?'

Just as she'd rehearsed, Jess took out a contract she'd typed earlier and handed it to him. Then she sat silently and forced herself to hold that benign smile Jared would.

As Kim studied the contract, Jess's heart was drumming so loudly in her ears, she feared he'd hear it from the other side of the table. The figure on the contract, to her eyes, looked horrendously expensive, but what it looked like to a man like Kim, she really had no idea. Jared had told her it was a bargain for the work involved and he insisted Kim would go for it, but . . .

She knew Kim had done his homework and that beneath his relaxed manner he was shrewd. She could see him weighing it up, hardly seeing it as the bargain Jared said it was, but not ruling it out, either. At one point he looked up at her, almost as if for guidance, and she forced herself not to say a word, not to move a muscle. *Just keep smiling*, she told herself.

She could feel the sweat pooling in the small of her back, but the poker tactics seemed to be working. She saw him waver, blow out his cheeks a little bit, as if giving in. Eventually, he put the contract on the coffee table, stood up and said, 'Let's eat, and come back to this.'

They sat on chrome stools at a high table in his well-appointed kitchen, and he proved to be a gourmet cook. 'I've been a bachelor too long,' he explained with a shy smile. He adjusted the lighting to a cosily intimate level and opened a good quality bottle of wine.

Jess allowed herself a sip, but no more — she had to stay sharp to close this deal. But after the tension in the living room, the chance to relax while they ate provided a respite that was intoxicating in itself.

Kim was good company and, once again, she found herself getting on well with him. So well, in fact, that she wished it was purely a social visit, without the background pressure of having to get a cheque out of him.

It turned out that he didn't come from the privileged background she had assumed. He came from a modest home, but had shown musical talent at an early age so his parents had made sacrifices to send him to a good music school. He won a scholarship to the Royal Academy of Music then found commercial success early. He'd acquired status through his own efforts. He really had no airs and graces at all and it was a shame, Jess thought, that he seemed to find it so hard meeting women who wanted him for who he was rather than what he had.

'Coffee?' he asked, and they sat in the kitchen and chatted some more.

He asked if she had anyone and she heard herself say, 'Sort of,' before admitting it was 'sort of' all in her mind and the guy she liked saw her as a friend but no more. She didn't know why she was telling Kim that, but it felt like a relief to tell somebody. He looked sympathetic and she was glad he didn't try to advise her.

Eventually, though, she guessed they both realised they'd been hiding in the kitchen too long, and so Kim made more coffee and they went back to the living room, where the contract waited on the coffee table

★ ★ ★

The romantic CD was long finished and Kim hadn't replaced it, the room growing so quiet that Jess could hear the clock ticking on the wall. She barely dared look at it. The coffee cups stood empty and Jess's face ached from holding a smile that had become a grimace and she was so drained she felt on the point of collapse.

Kim had asked so many questions she'd gone through almost the whole presentation again, but Jared had prepared her so thoroughly there wasn't one query she couldn't answer. Kim's cheque book lay open on the table, and his pen was in his hand, but still he hesitated, massaging his lower face with the hand that held the pen.

Don't speak, Jess told herself. Let it happen . . .

Eventually, Kim stood up with a sigh. He walked towards his piano and for a moment she thought he was going to start playing the bloomin' thing. He stopped in his tracks, rubbed the back of his neck, then turned around, came back across the room and sat down on the sofa beside her.

'The thing is, Jess . . . if I sign this, does that mean this will be the last time

I see you? Like we were this evening, I mean, over dinner.' He turned to face her, one hand on the back of the sofa, behind her. Then he started to lean in. 'Only I really would like to see you again . . . '

10

Jared sat slumped behind his desk and stared across the empty office. The window sash was still propped up on the book Jess had wedged there, and the late night sounds of the high street drifted in thinly, somehow emphasising the stillness.

PG Brachan had lied to him. It wasn't just Jared's office that was closing. Brachan had fed the same story to all the branches in the hope it would motivate the sales force to bring in enough cheques to stop the whole company going bankrupt. The plan hadn't worked, and when Brachan saw it wasn't working, he cashed what cheques had come in and did a runner. A lot of customers and a lot of salesmen were going to be left out of pocket.

When Jared got back from his

appointment, bailiffs were waiting to collect the keys to his company car. They carried out the phones, the computers and the filing cabinets before deciding the battered desks and chairs weren't worth taking.

The office itself was rented, so they let him keep the key. But they unscrewed and removed the sales board on which Jess and Jared were the only names still scrawled. All he had left was his bell, which was his personal property, although he had no cause to ring it.

He didn't tell the bailiffs where Jess had taken the other car, because he didn't want them to repossess it and leave her stranded. He said they'd have to come back for it on Monday. After making some calls on his mobile to people in other branches and ascertaining the full sorry situation, he tried to call Jess, but her phone was turned off. He tried to reach her via Kim Hunt's landline, but the number was permanently engaged.

He phoned Jess again and left another message. He hesitated to say what had happened, but decided he had to. He told her to meet him at the office as soon as her appointment was over. He said he'd wait for her, it didn't matter how late. After all the effort she had put in, only to have Brachan pull the carpet from beneath them at the last minute, he wanted to talk to her in person, not over the phone tomorrow. So he sat down and waited. And waited.

He spent the time thinking about Jess; everything they'd been through and all those little moments they'd shared together. He thought about that smile and just that way she had of being Jess. The thought of not seeing her again cut him deeper than anything else that had happened.

Long after he judged her appointment would have ended, he called her again, but her phone was still off — and Hunt's was still engaged. He wondered if she'd just gone home and hadn't bothered to check her messages, blissfully unaware that Brachan Windows was no more. She didn't have a landline, so he couldn't call her at home and he began to wonder if he'd be able to contact her before Monday.

He waited a while longer.

Eventually, he faced the probability that she hadn't got his message and wasn't coming. Or, worse, that she'd got his message and, since she no longer had a job, simply couldn't see the point in coming.

She'd call him tomorrow, he supposed, and go through the motions of asking if she'd get paid. He knew Jess wouldn't blame him — she'd know he wasn't going to get paid himself — but it would be awkward and painful, an empty parting he didn't want to think about.

With a heavy sigh, he toyed a moment with the office door key, reluctant to finally lock up and walk away from a place that had been his home for so long, reluctant to close the door on his time with Jess. She always made him feel so optimistic, like anything was possible. He wondered how he'd fare without her.

He decided to give her a few more minutes. Then he heard the clomp of a car door slamming in the yard downstairs.

★　★　★

Jess ran up the stairs, hot-cheeked and breathless. She'd got his message ages after he'd left it but her phone battery gave out before she could call him back. It was so late, she didn't think he'd still be here, but as she burst through the door and stood there, breathing hard, with her coat open over her little black Friday night dress and gathering herself after racing here so quickly, there he sat behind his desk, as calm and collected as ever.

For a long moment they just looked at each other. Eventually, he asked, gently, 'How did you get on?'

Physically and emotionally drained, she gave a small shrug. 'Some you win . . . ' She gave him a small smile and held up a cheque, fluttering slightly, between finger and thumb.

'You beauty!' Jared exclaimed. At that moment she could see he didn't give a stuff about the end of Brachan Windows. The cheque itself was irrelevant. He knew what it had meant to her to prove she could close the deal and the only thing that mattered to him was wanting to celebrate her achievement in its own right.

'Come here, sit down and tell me all about it,' he enthused.

'It's midnight,' Jess laughed.

'And your point is, Miss Watkins?'

So she flopped into the chair across the desk from him and, one sales pro to another, told him from the beginning. When she got to the bit about how much Kim had come on to her, his eyes widened.

'What happened?' he gasped.

'Well,' she said, coyly, 'I could have

played him along. You know, promised him dinner if he signed, then stall him once I had the cheque.'

'Would have taken a lot of stalling,' said Jared.

'That's what I thought. So I just looked him in the eye and calmly told him I wasn't part of the deal. If he still wanted to sign, that was fine, but if he didn't, that was fine, too. You should have felt the tension, because you have no idea how much I wanted that order, just to prove I could do it.'

'You've never had to prove anything to me,' he reproached her, gently and she could see the guilt on his face, for having put her in that position, albeit inadvertently.

'But the thing was,' Jess continued, 'Kim didn't know how much I wanted the order. And you know what he did? He just sort of smiled at me. Then he said, 'Okay, you win', picked up the pen and signed on the line. You should have seen how cool I was. I even let him make us some more coffee and we had a little chat, all good friends again, just to make sure there were no hard feelings because I didn't want him to change his mind and cancel the order the next day.

'It was only when I'd driven as far as the next road that I had to stop the car and scream, 'I've done it! I've done it!' I wanted to phone you and share it with you, didn't matter what time it was, and, of course, that's when I got your message.'

Jared looked almost tearful with pride and for once he just couldn't hide it. Having held back for so long, he stood up, gripped her shoulders and kissed her full on the lips.

Jess didn't so much see the kiss coming as felt the impulse in the same moment he did. As he left his seat, she stood also. Their lips met, softly and perfectly, but firmly and insistently.

Suddenly he was holding her tightly, clinging almost as if his life depended on her. She pushed her fingers through his soft hair and pressed him closer to her, their kiss deepening, neither wanting to break the contact between their lips.

Eventually — slowly, reluctantly, afraid they may never get to relive that moment again — their lips parted an inch or two, no more, their arms still entwined and they opened their eyes and gazed at each other.

Even more slowly, they let their arms drop until only their eyes still held onto each other. For a long moment, as they recovered their breath, neither spoke. Their lips had already said everything that needed to be said, and their eyes were still saying it.

Whether they sat silently like that for a minute or an hour, Jess had no idea. Eventually, when they both felt secure that their lives would be linked no matter what happened, Jared said light-heartedly, 'Shame we're both out of a job.'

'Apart from the fact that I don't have to feel quite so guilty about pinching one of PG's leads,' Jess said, mysteriously. She let the question mark hang on Jared's face for as long as was fair, before saying, 'You haven't read the cheque properly, have you? Or the contract.'

As Jared picked up the cheque, Jess stood up, slipped a sheaf of papers out of her file and handed it to him. While he looked from contract to cheque, she walked around the desk and stood behind him, reading over his shoulder.

'J J King Windows . . . ?' he said, in disbelief.

'The company you always wanted to start.' She rested her folded arms across the back of his shoulders, her chin just brushing his hair. 'You said we buy the actual windows from the factory, all we do is sell them. So, since it was becoming obvious we were finished here, I thought, well . . . I was afraid you might not want to do it, but I thought that if I got our first order, then you'd have to.'

Jared chuckled. 'I am so glad I

employed you, Jess.'

'Especially out of so many applicants, eh?' Jess said, teasingly. 'All with so much more experience and qualifications. How many were there?' Jared made a non-committal noise. 'Twenty . . . ?' Jess prompted. 'Ten . . . five . . . ?'

'Actually,' Jared confessed, 'You were the only one who turned up.'

For a long moment they both laughed at the absurdity of life and when their mirth petered out Jess felt secure enough to rest her cheek against his, revelling in the closeness of him.

Eventually, Jared said, 'You do realise, Miss Watkins, that we've got no office, no car, no phones, no computers . . . '

Jess straightened up, put her hands on his shoulders and began massaging knots of tension that had gone un-soothed for months, maybe years. 'And your point is, Mr King . . . ?'

It was then that Jared realised he still hadn't read the name on the contract properly. 'J J King? As in Jared and Jess?'

'If you'll have me.'

He leaned back, resting the back of his head against her torso and gave her an upside down smile.

'So who's the best, then?' Jess breathed.

As he mouthed his answer, she leaned forward and kissed him.

For a moment she thought he'd reached out and started ringing that bloomin' bell again, but then realised it was just the sound of church bells she was hearing — distant, but growing closer.

THE END

We do hope that you have enjoyed reading this large print book.

Did you know that all of our titles are available for purchase?

We publish a wide range of high quality large print books including:
Romances, Mysteries, Classics
General Fiction
Non Fiction and Westerns

Special interest titles available in large print are:
The Little Oxford Dictionary
Music Book, Song Book
Hymn Book, Service Book

Also available from us courtesy of Oxford University Press:
Young Readers' Dictionary
(large print edition)
Young Readers' Thesaurus
(large print edition)

For further information or a free brochure, please contact us at:
Ulverscroft Large Print Books Ltd.,
The Green, Bradgate Road, Anstey,
Leicester, LE7 7FU, England.
Tel: (00 44) **0116 236 4325**
Fax: (00 44) **0116 234 0205**

FINDING ANNABEL

Paula Williams

Annabel had disappeared after going to meet the woman who, she'd just discovered, was her natural mother . . . However, when her sister Jo travels to Somerset to try and find her, she must follow a trail of lies and deceit. The events of the past and the present have become dangerously entangled. And she discovers, to her cost, that for some people in the tiny village of Neston Parva, old loyalties remain fierce and strangers are not welcome . . .